Smith's MONTHLY

Every Month Original
Novels, Stories, and Articles

USA Today Bestselling Writer
Dean Wesley Smith

TABLE OF CONTENTS

Smith's Monthly Issue #11

Introduction
Stories Go On and On

STORIES FOR ME just seem to go on and on.

Not sure why that is. I have a Poker Boy short story in this issue that is part of an ongoing series. Poker Boy just seems to gain more and more powers with each new story I write about him. And let me tell you, there are a lot of Poker Boy stories. Plus there is one novel and a novella sequel to that novel.

Poker Boy just keeps going on and on.

And I have a Pilgrim Hugh story in this issue, the fourth one with that strange detective and his sidekicks. And I plan to write more because I kind of like that goofy detective. In fact, I can see a Pilgrim Hugh mystery novel in the near future.

And that novel will end up here in this magazine, of course.

The novel in this issue, *The High Edge*, is a Seeders Universe novel, the fifth novel in that series, actually. All of them were published in this magazine. And there will be more, since I actually know where the next novel will be set.

And with each Seeders novel, I am pulling all the main characters from each novel together more and more into a larger plot line, which for me has been great fun.

The Seeders Universe is a huge place, so lots of room to play and set fun stories.

In this issue, the two ongoing serial novels will both pass over 30,000 words in length. Each three-chapter segment in each issue for each story has been around 3,000 words long.

With Hawk, the story is far from over. I plan on just continuing on as Hawk looks for his father and the Fountain of Youth at the same time.

However, with Buffalo Jimmy, that book has a nice wrapping point for a novel in another couple of issues. So I may wrap that in a few more issues. And

Thanks for the Support

Dean Wesley Smith

then send him and his friends on another adventure. Time will tell on that.

I also have a series called "The Cold Poker Gang," of which I've had two stories and a novel in this magazine over this year, with more coming.

And last month I started a brand new series with the novel *Heaven Painted as a Poker Chip* novel.

I also have ten or more stories in my "Bryant Street" series, and about fifteen short stories in my Jukebox series.

Both of those series will continue on as well.

But the one series I like a great deal that started here in these pages is the "Thunder Mountain" series. There are three novels so far in the series, plus a number of short stories. The newest novel in the series will be out next month in these pages.

And speaking of going on and on, this magazine is only one month away from being in existence for a year. Without missing a month.

I fill every word of it. That sort of stuns my mind, to be honest, so I don't think about it much.

This issue is coming out in August, the month I started the Writing in Public challenge which set off this crazy magazine idea. If I was writing in public, I needed to have a place where readers could find most everything I wrote.

Eleven novels so far, counting this issue, with over forty-five short stories, two ongoing novels, and a nonfiction golf book.

This has been a really fun eleven months.

As with most of my fiction, the stories just keep going on and on, and this magazine shows no signs at all of slowing down either.

So next month will be the first year anniversary of *Smith's Monthly,* but this issue is the year anniversary of the challenge on my blog, Writing in Public.

And, as with any good series, I plan on going into year two with the challenge of Writing in Public.

So thanks for all the support over this last eleven months and I hope this has been fun and entertaining enough that you will join me for another year.

And maybe the year or two beyond that. As with most of the stories I write, I can see this magazine just going on and on.

I have no idea what will be coming in stories exactly, but I do have a lot of stories I want to write.

And I'm going to keep having fun.

Dean Wesley Smith
July 8, 2014
Lincoln City, Oregon

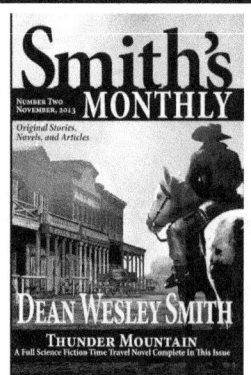

Coming Next Issue in Smith's Monthly
A Return to the Seeders Universe
in a brand new novel THE HIGH EDGE

Dean Wesley Smith

USA Today **Bestselling Writer**

A POKER BOY
STORY

DRIED UP

Asked in the middle of the night to help the dangerous race called Silicon Suckers, Poker Boy faces a challenge like none other.

He and Front Desk Girl risk their lives to help the alien-looking creatures, but then come face-to-face with what their bargain just might mean in the future.

DRIED UP
A Poker Boy Story

One

I VERY SELDOM get the feeling that something is wrong while sleeping beside Patty Ledgerwood, aka Front Desk Girl. In fact, until that very moment, it had never happened. Nothing ever seemed to be wrong when I was with Patty and not on a mission.

I get the "something-is-wrong" feeling at poker tables all the time, usually when another professional player is attempting to bluff me out of my shoes and all my money. I have learned to pay attention to that feeling, almost as if it is one of my superpowers. By paying attention, I have saved myself a ton of money over the years.

Right now I was in Patty's apartment near the University of Nevada, Las Vegas campus. In her master bedroom, to be exact. I could hear her regular breathing beside me, which told me she was sound asleep. The wonderful smell of her rose perfume filled the air and the feel of her expensive, fine-cotton sheets against my mostly bare skin felt wonderful, just as they always did.

Patty had had the day off, and we had spent it together; first at a movie, then a nice dinner at the buffet at the MGM Grand, and then back to her apartment to cuddle on the couch and watch television before heading to bed.

It didn't get much better these days.

But now, even without opening my eyes, I knew something was wrong.

I eased one eye open without moving, and couldn't see a thing in the dark room. The only light came from a nightlight in the bathroom to the right of the room and an alarm clock on the nightstand beside me. There was no light coming under the heavy curtains over the patio door, so it was still dark outside as well.

I eased over to glance at the time, and a lightning storm went off in the sheets.

And that wasn't a metaphor for some sexual thing.

A real lightning storm erupted around me, as more static electricity than I could imagine let loose.

And each spark was like a kid pinching me. Let me tell you, the sparks hurt.

"Wow!" I said out loud as I sat up.

It was as if I had rubbed my entire body across a carpet and then was touching things.

My movement caused the sheets to explode with even more static electricity which woke Patty up, and she sat bolt upright in bed as well, causing even *more* sparks as she sat stunned at the light show going on around us.

And the tiny pinches of pain with every large spark.

Somehow, every bit of moisture had been sucked out of the room, and a very large, background, static electric charge had filled the air.

"Sit still," I said, as Patty moved slightly and the room lit up with a light show once again.

"Ouch!" Patty said, freezing in place. "That hurts."

I had heard of many reasons for friction in bed, but this was ridiculous.

But in the light caused by the sparks with Patty's last movement, I had seen the problem.

Two alien-looking creatures with large black eyes and oblong heads stood at the end of the bed, staring at us.

It was like a scene out of a bad alien-abduction movie.

The UFO conspiracy people called them "Grays," but I knew them to be members of a race native to Earth called the Silicon Suckers.

In fact, they had been around far, far longer than humans.

They hate water and could deal with very little if any of it. Clearly they took what water they needed right out of the air around them.

They lived in very dry caves in the desert. The caves were so dry, the air would kill a human after just a couple of days, even with enough drinking water, which wasn't allowed in the homes of the Silicon Suckers.

Their very presence in Patty's apartment had sucked all the moisture out of the room.

I had never heard of a Silicon Sucker being seen inside a human city. Something had to be very, very wrong.

I carefully motioned for Patty to look at the foot of the bed. The sparks from my slight movement bit into me again and lit up the room.

She saw them and her breath sucked in with surprise. She instinctively pulled the sheet up to her neck covering up her nightgown and causing a large electrical storm around her and me.

Damn those little sparks hurt. It was lucky we just didn't burst into flames right there.

"Sorry," she said, holding her breath against the pain.

I had dealt with the Silicon Suckers a number of times before, and been in their sacred caves they called "sand castles." I had always been welcomed in their world because of a couple of favors I had done for them over the last few years.

"Greetings, honored guests," I said, bowing my head slightly and hoping the movement wouldn't set the sheets on fire. "What do I owe this great honor?"

Both Silicon Suckers bowed in return. Both looked identical. The one on the right spoke.

"Poker Boy, Front Desk Girl, we ask for your assistance in a matter of importance to our people."

"Of course," I said.

Both Patty and I bowed slightly.

After the sparks stopped I said, "It will be a great honor to help our friends."

Both again bowed in acceptance. "Our leader will speak to you at sunrise."

"We will attend," I said, also bowing again and setting off even more sparks. This room was going to need a humidifier real quick or we would be calling for fire trucks.

Without another word, the two turned and went out through curtains covering the bedroom's patio door, setting off a huge wave of sparks. I knew for a fact that the door had been locked and secured when we had gone to bed.

I had no idea how they had gotten in, or how they would get from Patty's apartment near UNLV, across town, actually across the Strip, and back into the desert.

The moment the curtains dropped back into place in a shower of static electricity, I instantly transported us into the living room area of Patty's apartment. The air there felt dry, but nothing like the intense lack of moisture in the bedroom.

I loved my newly learned superpower of teleportation. I just never expected to use it teleporting out of Patty's bed.

Patty used a napkin to flip on a light, took one look at me and started to laugh.

Now trust me, a beautiful woman in a sheer blue nightgown laughing when she sees your almost-naked body does not do wonders for even my superhero ego.

But I had to admit she looked just as funny. Besides all the tiny red marks all over her arms and wonderful legs that showed under her nightgown, her long brown hair stuck out in all directions from her head like she had been attacked by a mad hairdresser. Her hair was spread so wide, I doubt she could even get through a door.

And her wonderful face looked like it had a bad case of measles.

I glanced down at my own legs and chest, also covered with hundreds and hundreds of small red marks, as if I had been attacked by a swarm of bed bugs. Then I felt my brown hair, which was also standing straight out in all directions. And I could also feel my face was covered in the tiny red bumps from the electrical shocks.

Thank heavens I had worn my boxers to bed. The thought of electronic shocks to certain parts of my body just made me shudder.

Two

AFTER WE CAREFULLY opened the windows and doors to let in some of what now seemed like balmy and humid Las Vegas summer air, we both drank three large glasses of water.

Thirsty didn't begin to describe what I was feeling.

Then, when we both had extra-large glasses of water in our hands, I shouted at the ceiling. "Stan. Need help!"

I have no idea how he always heard me, but he always did. Stan was the God of Poker, and my immediate boss.

An instant later he appeared in Patty's living room in front of us, looking grumpy

that I had disturbed him in the middle of the night. He normally wore brown slacks, a light sweater, and black shoes. He was a short man, not even close to my six-foot height, and I seldom saw him smile. His dark hair was cut very short all the time, and his eyes looked almost black.

But tonight he had on a white golf shirt and blue golf shorts and the shorts looked like they were on backwards. When the God of Poker can't even dress himself, he really was tired.

He started to say something, then took one look at us and started laughing. I had seen him laugh a few times, but when a god starts to laugh at you, it is always worrisome.

But I had to admit that we did look funny. There was no containing our hair and the red marks on our faces, arms, and legs were getting brighter by the second.

"You two go through a swarm of bees on a rollercoaster?"

"Nope," I said as he laughed. "Just an electrical storm in bed."

He started to make some joke, then looked at Patty, then back at me and couldn't say anything because he was laughing too hard.

"I'm not kidding," I said. "Two Silicon Suckers woke us up and asked for our help."

Stan's laughing instantly vanished and he went back to his normal poker face. His golf shirt and golf shorts instantly became his normal slacks and sweater and black shoes.

It seemed I now had his attention and he was very much awake.

"How in the world did they get here?" he asked, shaking his head. "And when are you supposed to meet them?"

"We are meeting their leader at sunrise."

"You are meeting the Great One?"

Now he was stunned and when he said it like that, it bothered me as well. Patty just looked worried under all the red marks and massive head of hair spread out three feet around her head. It was going to take her some real time once the static charge faded to untangle all that wonderful long hair.

"You ever heard of the Silicon Suckers coming into any human town?" I asked Stan. "Just to ask for human help?"

"Never," he said, shaking his head.

"Have you heard any rumors about anything going wrong in their caves? Or anyone having a run-in with them?"

"Nothing," he said, "but I might have missed something. Stay put, I'm going to go get Burt and maybe Laverne."

He vanished.

Laverne was Lady Luck herself, in charge of all of the gambling and gaming universe. Burt was her second in command. I'd been around Lady Luck a number of times now, and Patty and I and the team had actually saved her life once. But she still scared hell out of me.

If Stan thought this was worth waking up Burt and maybe even Laverne, then Patty and I really might be in over our heads. We were just lowly superheroes.

Really dry and marked-up superheroes.

I had just taken another drink of water and was about to suggest we get a little more dressed when Laverne and Stan appeared. Lady Luck had on a strict brown business suit with her brown hair pulled back tight in a bun. She did not look happy.

When she saw us she raised one eyebrow, but did not smile, even though we looked really, really silly. With a wave of her hand Patty and I were both dressed,

the static gone from our hair and the red marks gone from our skin.

Patty in her normal black pants and white blouse. Laverne had put me in my normal jeans with dress shirt, black leather coat and Fedora-like black hat. That was my poker uniform.

"Thank you," Patty said.

I nodded agreement. "Yes, thank you. I feel much better."

I could also feel the extra power that my coat and hat brought to me from the nearby casinos.

"No idea at all what the Silicon Suckers want?" Lady Luck asked, all business.

"Not a clue," I said. "Has something like this ever happened before?"

"Never," she said. "I have only met The Great One once, a few thousand years ago. But I do know that he only concerns himself with matters of major importance."

"I wonder why he came to us instead of you?" Patty asked. "It makes no sense."

"He didn't want to bother you," I said to Lady Luck, knowing the answer to Patty's question. "This is something he feels Patty and I can accomplish."

Both Laverne and Stan nodded.

"That makes sense," Laverne said. "But it gets us no closer to what he might want. And we just don't have time to figure it out. You had better get going."

"We have one stop to make first," I said.

I turned to my direct boss. "Stan, could you get me six thermoses and two backpacks to carry them in, and meet me at The Diner?"

Stan nodded and vanished.

"Good luck," Laverne said. "If you need my help in any fashion, just call out. I will be standing by."

"Thank you," Patty said as Laverne vanished.

I glanced at Patty, who looked stunning, as always, in the dark slacks and white blouse that Laverne had dressed her in. Her brown hair was combed and under control. Only the worry showing in her dark-brown eyes flawed the picture.

"Ready for an adventure?" I asked.

"With you, always," she said, smiling.

I took her hand and jumped us to The Diner, our favorite restaurant and meeting place tucked off on a side street in downtown Las Vegas. It was a place decorated in a fake 1960s look and run by Madge, a superhero in the food service part of the world. Madge seemed to always be there and she made the best milkshakes on the planet.

Ten minutes later, Madge and Stan had us ready to go and we jumped to the outskirts of Las Vegas near a huge Las Vegas billboard.

Three

THE COOL MORNING desert air hit my face and I was glad to have the leather jacket on.

Patty had over one shoulder a backpack with three thermoses of hot chocolate, and I had the other backpack on my back with the other three.

Hot chocolate was like an extreme drug to the Silicon Suckers. One single drop of the liquid would send a Sucker into a drug high that seemed to last for a long time.

I had learned a long time ago to never think of going into one of the Silicon Sucker cities without a gift of a thermos of hot chocolate. And since we were going to see the Great One, it made sense to carry even more of the gift.

We had arrived fifteen minutes ahead of our time to meet the Great One, but I had a hunch it would take us that long to get to where he was through the vastness of the underground city. The sun had already lit up the hills and desert with a golden glow and the air still had an early-morning chill to it that promised to be gone very shortly in the summer heat.

"You ready?" I asked.

Patty nodded, but looked very nervous. She had never been inside a Silicon Sucker "sand castle" as they liked to call their huge network of caves and tunnels in the sandstone and rock.

While the hot chocolate was being made, Stan had briefed Patty on all the rules of the Silicon Sucker city.

We could never touch a wall. We could never sit down unless invited. We had to always treat the Suckers with respect by bowing. We had to give our full and honest name before being allowed to enter. And so on and so on. They were a very rule-bound race.

I had us face directly east, then, to the seemingly open-air twenty paces from the big billboard, I said, "Poker Boy and Front Desk Girl ask for entrance into the great city of the Silicon Suckers."

The entrance of a large tunnel shimmered into existence in front of us. It seemed to go into the side of a hill that just didn't appear to be there. Very weird.

I slipped off my shoes, leaving them on the desert sand. Patty did the same, and we stepped forward into the tunnel that slanted downward gently.

About twenty paces inside we were met by a Silicon Sucker who bowed as we bowed and gave our full names.

"Welcome to our castle once again, Poker Boy," he said. "It is always an honor to have you as a guest."

He turned to Patty. "It is also an honor to have you visit our castle."

"The honor is all mine," Patty said, bowing slightly.

With all the greetings done, the Silicon Sucker turned and indicated we should follow him.

As I had guessed, it seemed to take a long time for us to reach the major cavern and work our way down one wall on sloping ramps. For a person afraid of heights, this path on the face of the wall would be pure hell. It was a long ways down and there were no guardrails and you weren't allowed to touch the wall on the inside.

The cavern seemed to stretch into the distance and the walls were riddled with paths and open tunnels. They seemed to be crawling with Silicon Suckers.

I had never seen so many out and moving at the same time before. I felt like I had been shrunk down and was walking in an anthill.

The floor of the huge cavern had hundreds and hundreds of buildings and I knew from earlier visits that the caverns and tunnels went deep under all the buildings as well.

Seeing so many Silicon Suckers moving at once, I suddenly wondered what all of them ate and how so many could be fed? No doubt I dare not ask such a question.

I glanced at Patty who was following me. She seemed to be doing fine as we went down the wall face, even in the drying air. I could feel the moisture in my lips and skin drying up and the leather jacket I wore didn't feel so comfortable now in the growing heat. But I didn't dare take it off, not only because it would be an insult in the city, but it gave me extra power. And there was no telling what I might need to do in this situation.

The deeper we got into the city, the drier the air got. We could not bring any kind of water with us. Plain drinking water was forbidden in a Silicon Sucker castle.

These places were very, very dangerous to humans. I knew of one superhero who had managed three days in a Silicon Sucker castle negotiating with them on some land swap, but she had barely made it out alive.

We reached the cavern floor and headed toward the huge center building. There was nothing ornate about it and no windows at all. It seemed more like a giant mound of sand. But it was the largest building and it did seem to be in the center of the cavern, which I was sure had some significance.

We were led inside and into a large, domed room with no furniture of any kind. It seemed to be the very center of the large mound of sand that was this building.

The floor was nothing but hard sand, warm under my bare feet, and the walls were brown like everything else in these underground cities. It looked like the special rooms weren't any more decorated than any of the other rooms in this cavern.

The Silicon Sucker who led us into the room indicated we should stand and wait and then he left.

There was only one other door into the room, an archway on the other side. We both stood, facing that doorway, not talking.

I could feel beads of sweat forming on my face and then drying away almost instantly.

I always got scared inside these cities. After all, Silicon Suckers looked just like every alien I had seen in the movies. That fear was very deep in all humans, more than likely from centuries around this race.

Honestly, at the moment I was more scared than I had ever been before.

If Laverne had only met the Great One once in thousands of years, why were we standing here?

And how many ways could we make a mistake and never see the light of the desert above again?

Suddenly, in front of us, a Silicon Sucker entered the room completely alone. As with all of them, he wore nothing, but he moved slower than the rest, and as he got closer to us, I could see his bright red eyes. And his face looked longer than the rest. But otherwise, besides the red eyes, I would have never been able to tell the Great One from any other Silicon Sucker.

Patty and I both bowed to him and he returned the bow.

"I thank you for this audience," he said, his voice strong and commanding.

"It is an honor to be asked," I said.

Patty and I both bowed again slightly.

"We have brought gifts, if you would allow us."

He held up his hand for us to not move, and we both stood still.

"I thank you for the gifts," the Great One said, "but I must first talk to you about why I asked you here. My people find themselves in a problem of our own making."

Patty and I carefully said nothing.

"It seems that the gifts you have brought us in the past, and the regular payment for the land we have exchanged, has brought us to a crisis point."

He paused and then looked down as if embarrassed.

I knew he was talking about hot chocolate. Over the last few years I had brought his people six thermoses full. And for a piece of land they were getting ten thermoses every month. I knew that hot chocolate was a very powerful drug to the Silicon Suckers, but I couldn't imagine it becoming a crisis.

Then it hit me. *A powerful drug!*

Could he be mad at me for getting his people hooked on hot chocolate? Had I created a drug problem in his perfectly ordered world? No wonder he wanted to only "talk" with me.

But why had he also asked Patty to come along? Was it because she was special to me and he needed to take something special of mine for what I had done to his people?

I would not allow that.

The Great One looked up at me, the large unblinking red eyes clear.

"Poker Boy," he said, "I do not think you understand the value of your gracious gifts to my people. Your precious gifts give us life and energy. It gives us an excitement that we have not felt in many, many centuries."

I somehow managed to keep my mouth shut and just let him continue. I needed to be ready, if this turned very ugly, to jump Patty and me out of here quickly, or call for Lady Luck to come to our rescue.

The Great One continued.

"Your gifts have allowed me to walk out here without being carried and to stand here as a leader once again."

Now I was staring at him and my eyes suddenly felt like they were as wide as his were.

"Our problem is that our numbers are increasing with the new vitality from your gifts and land payments. And each cycle the payment for the land is not enough to supply my people."

Suddenly the fear I had been feeling turned to barely-controlled panic.

He wasn't mad at me for bringing the gifts of hot chocolate. This was much, much worse.

He needed *more* of it.

Oh, crap. I couldn't just offer it to him as a gift. I would insult him, and more than likely we would die where we stood.

I needed to find a way, and find it quickly, to get the Silicon Suckers more hot chocolate and let the Great One feel as if he was paying a fair price.

I nodded and somehow, keeping my voice from cracking in the dry air, I said, "A great leader worrying about the well-being of his people. It is an honor to be in your presence."

I took the pack from my shoulder and took out the three thermoses, holding them in my hands and not allowing even the pack to touch the ground.

Beside me, Patty followed my lead and did the same.

"For the honor of meeting with the Great One," I said, "the leader of all Silicon Suckers, we have brought this special gift. I hope it will help while we work out a more lasting solution and a fair and equitable trade."

"I can only thank you for your generosity," he said.

Without any indication of a movement from the Great One, six other Silicon Suckers came out and each took one thermos and carried them away like carrying gold from the room.

After they had left I spoke again.

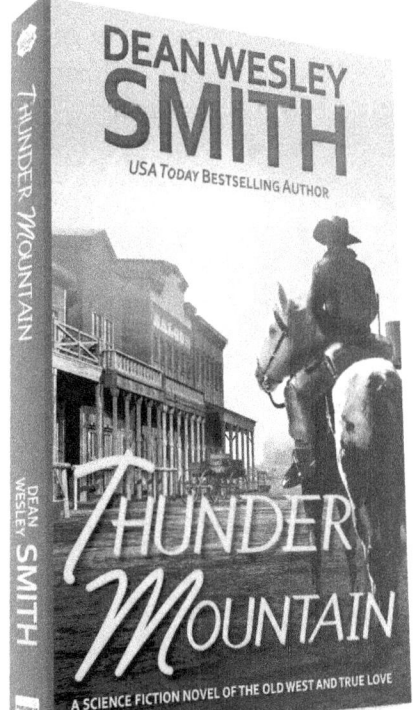

"May I be so bold as to ask how much of the precious substance is needed to supply the great beings of the race of Silicon Suckers with their needs?"

He stared at me for a moment and I began to wonder if I had gone too far with my question.

Then he said, "We would need four times the amount of your generous gift every moon cycle, plus the payment for the land we are already receiving."

I tried to look serious. Thirty-four thermoses full of hot chocolate. "That is a large amount," I said. "But it is possible. But I must ask for something in return."

"Of course," he said.

I had an idea on what we might trade for, but I had to be very careful in presenting it.

"My people are also in great need in this area for…" I stopped and looked pained. "…I am sorry, I cannot use such language in front of the Great One."

He motioned for me to continue.

"We are in need of plain water. We are a very different people, with different needs. We must have plain water to survive. Is there an area in your lands which is not usable to your people because of too much plain water that we might trade?"

"Something important to my people in exchange for something important to your people," he said.

I only nodded. Thankfully he saw my purpose and I had not insulted him by asking for what was, in essence, poison to his people.

"Poker Boy, there is a reason my people sing your praises."

"Thank you, Great One," I said.

A map of the area around Las Vegas appeared in the air between us. Some areas were colored in gold for Silicon Sucker lands. Black for human lands. Gray for land that neither party controlled.

I knew the Silicon Suckers protected their own lands fiercely when needed, and no building was allowed within one hundred yards of any border to their property.

Of course, no humans in Las Vegas government knew that. The map had been formed by treaty decades before by the Gods of Land Use and the Silicon

Suckers. The gods in that area made sure nothing was allowed to be built on the Silicon Sucker lands.

The Great One pointed to a small area colored red off to one side of the old Boulder Dam highway. It did not seem to be attached to any other area of Silicon Sucker lands.

"We were forced to abandon a growing castle in this area due to large pools of the evil liquid under the area. I would like five times your most recent gift every moon cycle in trade for the entire area."

He had upped the amount expecting me to bargain. Again, I needed to not insult him by giving in too quickly.

"Forty containers of the precious liquid every moon cycle?" I asked.

He said simply, "Yes."

I pointed at the large area of red off the old highway. "My people will find much of what we need here?"

"You will find much of the poison there," he said.

I didn't want to tell him that the precious liquid he was asking for was based on the poison we called water.

"Twenty-eight additional every moon cycle," I said. "And if we find what we must look for on the land, we will increase the amount to forty total in twelve moon cycles."

He nodded. "Your terms are acceptable."

The red coloring of the land on the map turned to blue and then the map vanished.

"The first payment will be delivered tomorrow morning," I said, "to the area near the entrance to this castle at sunrise, and then at sunrise every moon cycle after."

The Great One bowed and Patty and I bowed also.

"This exchange has given my people a new beginning," he said. "It will allow my people to reproduce and spread and build many large new castles. You will both always be honored guests as long as I rule."

With that he turned and walked away.

For a moment I felt the elation that we had survived the meeting. Then his last words came back strong, like someone was shouting them in my head.

Hot chocolate helped these creatures have baby Silicon Suckers?

Wow, I had not known that. No wonder I had never seen any children. I had never thought of it before.

What had I just done?

Patty and I followed a guide out of the building and back up the wall toward the entrance above. All the paths and tunnels teamed with Silicon Suckers, far, far more than I had ever seen before.

Was all this population growth from just a few thermoses per month of hot chocolate?

Oh, man, what would forty every month do?

What had I done?

Was I setting up a future war between mankind and Silicon Suckers? I sure hoped not.

Outside, after Patty kissed me for a job well done and we put on our shoes in the already hot sun, I told her my worry.

She just laughed in that way she does that makes me relax. It's one of her very special superpowers I'm sure.

Then she said, "I could really use a couple glasses of water and a large breakfast."

"You don't think this is serious, do you?"

"They don't dare expand into our areas and fight with us."

"And why not?" I asked as I jumped us from the hot desert to our favorite booth in the air-conditioning of The Diner. I didn't want to call for Stan and Laverne until I understood what Patty was saying.

"There weren't that many of them moving around last time I was down there," I said as we slid into the booth, the cool vinyl seat feeling wonderful. "That's only after six months of regular hot chocolate use. Imagine after a year?"

Again Patty laughed. "Trust me, they have to treat us well."

"And why?" I asked as Madge headed our way with large glasses of water she must have had ready.

"Because if they don't," Patty said, patting my hand on the table top like I was two years old, "we just cut off their supply of hot chocolate."

"Oh," was all I could think to say.

~

Now Available
from all your favorite booksellers
in trade paper and electronic editions.

USA *Today* Bestselling Writer
DEAN WESLEY SMITH

It's a Mystery Story...

WELL, MAYBE NOT

"One event follows another." I remember saying that up on a writing panel one day and then added in "Well, maybe not."

That stuck with me and I went back and decided to start with an event and see what happened if I ended the event with "Well, maybe not."

This may well be one of the strangest stories I have ever written. Well, maybe not...

WELL, MAYBE NOT

One

CHANNEL SURFING was Henry's life.

Click.

Jackie "Big Tits" Simpson slipped seductively up to the counter of Chucky Cheese and leaned forward just enough to cause her low-cut sweater to bag open the right amount. As the newest star of the famous soap opera "Eat Me," this was her big moment.
Her big break.
Her best shot at showing off her big tits.
"May I help you?" the fat kid with the pimples on his nose asked. He stood back a few feet as if he were afraid to get too close to Jackie, but in actuality it was to make sure all eyes remained on her.
"You sure can," she said and then slowly, oh, so slowly, she turned to face the camera...

Click.

Jill Bantor, bartender extraordinaire, flipped the bottle high into the air and caught it with her perfect right hand, the bottle's spout poised perfectly over the highball glass, ready to pour the perfect martini, not too wet, not too dry.

Harvey, her boss, the love of her life, watched from his usual seat.

Tonight she would get him to her pink, padded bed.

Get those tight pants off those wonderful buns.

Get him to....

Click.

Henry sucked down another handful of way-too-salty chips and clicked past five shopping channels. He loved to channel surf, loved to spend the evening just catching slight glimpses of other worlds.

He'd sit in his small two-bedroom-with-one-bath ranch house every night, seven days a week, surfing. Dishes would pile up in the sink and he wouldn't notice until the flies got too bad.

His laundry would go unwashed for weeks until he ran out of socks. Empty bags of potato chips would surround his couch until he couldn't stand kicking them out of the way.

He'd surfed for years and now that they had improved the cable channels he had even more choices.

"Cindy Slut, private dick, will return after a message from our sponsor Magic Hot Tubs."

Henry was about to surf on when on the forty-inch screen appeared a naked, sloppy, fat man with a very small penis. So small it took a close-up shot with a ground level camera focused up to even see it.

Henry watched, arm poised, special surfing control aimed at the set ready to move on as the fat guy huffed and grunted and finally shifted his bulk over the edge of the blue hot tub and settled into the bubbling water. Below the picture flashed off and on the words "Hidden camera view of satisfied customer."

Water splashed over the edge of the tub and after a moment the man's eyes seemed to roll up into his head.

Below the picture the words switched to "ten minutes elapsed time" and the picture shifted slightly as what appeared to be the same man shook his head, stretched and then stood up.

He was now slim, with a deep tan, a handsome grin, and a huge penis. So big the camera had to pull back to catch it all.

"Wow!" Henry said and scrambled for a pen to write down the toll-free number.

Henry was clearly overweight and his dick at its best was no longer than his little finger, even though he always thought of himself as just average. This Magic Hot Tub would be the perfect thing for him.

He would buy the Magic Hot Tub, soak in it for ten minutes and never have to diet again. And he could meet women and do things to them that he couldn't even see done on the Penthouse channel.

And then afterwards they could channel surf together, of course, with him holding the control.

He reached for the phone. This would be great.

Well, maybe not.

Two

DETECTIVE Danny Dohickey stared down at the bloated, overcooked form of Henry floating in the steaming water. So far the flies hadn't started swarming, but it would only be another hour or so. They had been lucky to get the call from the meter man on this one. Sometimes these hot tub deaths went days without being discovered. Usually the neighbors complained about the smell after three days.

"Another Magic Hot Tub death?" his partner, Detective Walter Waker asked as he glanced at the body, his face showing the disgust he felt and the indigestion from too much pork at breakfast.

"Afraid so," Danny said.

"Why anyone would use these things is beyond me," Walter said. He leaned over the edge and looked at the special box on the side. "Penis enlarger again?"

"Afraid so," Danny said.

"Another one cut off?"

"Afraid so." Danny pointed to the shriveled, finger-looking thing floating near the filter.

"Medical examiner done with him?"

"Afraid so."

"Which means we've got to haul him out of there?"

"Afraid so."

Walter rolled up his sleeves, reached in, and grabbed a leg.

Danny grabbed an arm and they heaved and hauled and huffed and puffed and after a good ten minutes they had flopped Henry like a dead white fish beside the tub.

"You as wet as I am?" Walter asked, brushing water from his arms and pants.

"Afraid so," Danny said.

"He's all yours," Walter said to the woman from the morgue. "We got a report to fill out, don't we Danny?"

"Afraid so."

Betty Black, the woman from the morgue, put the cart beside Henry and gestured to the two cops. "Not before you roll him onto there." She pointed to her cart.

She wasn't going to do it and hurt her back. She needed her back limber for what she had planned later that night.

Walter grunted, but both detectives quickly had Henry on the cart and were walking away.

Suddenly Walter turned back to Betty. "Forgot to tell you. His penis is still in the hot tub."

"You're kidding!" Betty said.

This was her first Magic Hot Tub death and she hadn't heard about what really happened from reading the papers.

"Afraid not," Walter said, obviously enjoying her discomfort.

"And I have to fish it out?"

Afraid so," Danny said, slapped his partner on the back. Laughing, they walked off.

"Wonderful," Betty said in disgust, staring down at the naked, penis-less fat man on her stretcher. "And I'll bet it was a big one, too."

Well, maybe not.

Three

BETTY USUALLY WORE black to work. She felt it appropriate, since she worked with so much death. But at work in the morgue they always made her put on a clean, white surgical gown over her street clothes.

Betty was a pretty average woman, both in size and looks and the white surgical gown did nothing to help those looks. It flattened her chest and covered her best asset, her ass.

Betty had only worked at the morgue for three weeks, but her years of training were medical. And some veterinary. But that was much earlier.

Now she was in line for helping out with autopsies. That had been a dream of hers since the first time she had cut open her brother's dead dog to see how much damage the car had done.

"You want this one to be your first?" Brad, Betty's boss, asked her, pointing at the naked Harry with his small penis laying on the stretcher beside him. "You could do him this afternoon and I could watch."

Brad's face seemed almost flushed and he sounded breathless.

Betty almost clapped her hands together in excitement. Her first. She was really looking forward to cutting this one open, stem to stern, then talking into the recorder about what she was seeing, and then doing the report. It was what she had trained all these years for, the ultimate moment.

"That would be wonderful," she said to Brad, doing her best to keep her voice in control and totally professional.

Brad nodded and smiled real big. "Good. But lunch first. I know this great Italian place with the best red sauce and big glasses of wine. I'll meet you outside in five minutes."

"Wonderful," Betty said and watched Brad head toward his office. Too bad he was married, she always thought when she watched him walk away from her. This time was no exception to that rule.

As Brad left, she turned to face the naked form of Henry.

"Well, it seems you get to be the lucky one." She patted his fat, cold stomach and then walked around the table. "You get to be my first real stiff, not like those in school. You get to be the one who pops my cherry."

Henry, of course, didn't say a word.

"You know," she said, "I need something to remember this day. Maybe I should buy myself a special present. What do you think about that?"

Again, of course, Henry didn't say a word. He was just too dead.

"Or maybe I should keep a little something from inside of you."

She pretended to make a cut mark down the center of his chest.

Henry kept very still, as was his condition.

"But Brad will be here then. Maybe I should just take this."

She picked up Henry's small (and now-even-smaller-because-the-water-had-shrunk-it) penis.

She held it up in front of her face, turning it to look at all sides, studying the pattern of wrinkles. "I think this will be a wonderful memento, don't you?"

Henry would have objected, of that there was no doubt, but he couldn't and therefore didn't.

So Betty pulled off her surgical gown, opened her black handbag and dropped Henry's penis into her change purse.

"Thanks," she said and patted Henry's arm. "I've got a wonderful lunch date, but I will see you this afternoon."

Well, maybe not.

Four

BETTY AND BRAD had three large glasses of wine each and both were feeling very, very happy.

Brad had suggested she do Henry in the private cutting room, with the door locked so that they wouldn't be interrupted. Betty had been so excited at that suggestion she almost wet herself.

On the way back, both of them breathless, both excited, both half smashed, they didn't expect a problem.

But they got one.

A big one.

The city bus with the bad brakes that none of the bus drivers wanted to drive, jumped the curb and gave both Betty and Brad a very quick ride into the side of a brick three-story building.

Blood splattered everywhere and the clean-up crew ended up having an awful time telling which part went with which body. However, a few hours later Betty and Bob were both beside Harry again, in body bags, smaller bags, and buckets. Not at all the way they had intended.

Betty's black handbag was tossed clear of the massive mess and mayhem, where it was picked up by a homeless young woman from Kansas named Dot. She held it for a time, watching the cops and medics clean up the mess, pretending all the time that she would give the handbag to the first person who asked.

She stood there for an hour, pretending.

But no one asked, so she decided she would turn it in later.

Back at her hot-air grate beside the dumpster, she opened the bag and found eighteen dollars in bills. She also saw a picture of Betty's apartment and in a secret place inside the lining she found a naked picture of Betty with her legs spread. Why Betty would carry a picture of herself doing that was beyond Dot, who was from a farm and had never really even looked at herself naked in a mirror. When she was growing up she even locked her dog out of the bathroom when she was taking a bath.

Inside the change purse was another eighty-seven cents and a strange-looking rubbery thing.

"Oh, yuck," she said and dropped the thing back inside the handbag with the picture of naked Betty.

She dug through the rest of the junk in the bag, but found nothing worth anything at all. She stuffed the money into a deep pocket in her cloth coat and held the bag at arm's length and looked at it. "Maybe I can get a reward for this down at the police station."

Well, maybe not.

Five

THE BIG GUY with a gray mustache behind the desk at the police station just took the purse after listening to Dot's story. He sort of grunted a thank you and then handed the purse to a young woman in a freshly ironed and washed uniform behind him. "Run this to the morgue to be put with the other personal stuff of that woman bus-crash victim."

The young woman named Officer Josepha Friday nodded her head excitedly, like a little puppy, then scampered forward and took the bag. "Yes, sir. Will do, sir."

The desk sergeant rolled his eyes as she ran at top speed for the back door of the station that would lead across the alley to the morgue.

But she didn't have to run far.

In that alley waited postal worker Ken Silverman, who was angry at his wife, his boss, and the fact that his best friend had been arrested by the police for the sixth time for drunk driving. Because of that, Ken's friend had lost his job.

So while sorting letters, Ken decided to do something about everything. He went home that afternoon, early, without telling anyone and immediately got in a fight with his wife, took out the pistol he had bought for her to protect herself coming home on bridge night, and shot her in the chest three times.

Then he reloaded, went back down to the post office and shot his boss, then calmly walked downtown to the police station where he waited in the alley until Josepha came out.

He told her to stop.

She saw his gun and reached for hers. She had just been trained last month to do the draw and she knew how to do it real well.

But she never really got to it.

He shot her.

Twice.

Two hours later Betty's handbag ended up in Josepha's personal stuff in a locker in the morgue. And there it seemed destined to stay.

Well, maybe not.

Six

THE NEXT MORNING Jill, Josepha's twin sister, arrived at the morgue with her husband Jack Hill. Jill had obviously been crying all night and

it took everything Jack could do to keep her from tumbling to the floor in a pile as she looked at poor Josepha laid out there on the slab, two holes punched in her chest and a look of surprise stuck on her face.

After all the viewing and crying and stuff was over, the night guy at the morgue, who had suddenly been promoted to the day guy, handed Jill her sister's box of personal things. Jill thanked him and without even looking at what was in the box left the morgue.

At home that night, in front of a crackling fire, she got up the nerve to open the box.

Inside was Josepha's uniform with two holes in it.

Her bra, also with two holes in it, but these holes were designed by the manufacturer and Jill was shocked. She quickly hid the bra so Jack wouldn't see it. She didn't want him to get any ideas.

Little did she know that Jack knew about the holes in Josepha's bra, and much more, too. He had spent many a night peeking into Jill's sister's bedroom window when he had told his wife he was out jogging. He always came home sweating, so she believed him.

Jill found no underwear in the box, but some nylons and lace garters. There was an envelope with the contents of Josepha's pockets in it. Just some change and a wine opener.

So Jill opened the big black handbag and the first thing she pulled out was the picture of a naked Betty.

"Oh my God," Jill said.

"Something I can do, dear," Jack said as he came in from the kitchen and looked over her shoulder. Before Jill could hide the picture he too gasped. "Who's that?"

"I don't know," Jill said.

Jill dropped the picture on the carpet and looked carefully into the purse. And there she saw this finger-long piece of shriveled skin and meat.

With her fingernails she gently picked it out of the purse and held it up. "What is—?"

"My God!" Jack said. "It's a man's penis!"

Jill screamed, dropped the penis into the bag, and then fainted.

Jill had never seen a man's penis, not even Jack's, since they "did it" in the dark.

Twenty minutes later she still hadn't come to, so Jack called an ambulance and ten minutes after that they were speeding toward the hospital, forgetting a few things such as the handbag on the living room floor, Jill's own much smaller purse on the stand beside the front door, and locking the back door.

Outside Bad Boy Benny Burges, the fifteen-year-old neighborhood bully and drug pusher watched the scene as they rushed Jill from the house to the ambulance.

He smiled to himself and ambled slowly down the tree-lined street as the ambulance sped off. He went an entire block before cutting through to the alley and then back to the rear of Jill's house.

He smiled even bigger when he discovered the back door was unlocked.

And he broke out into an even bigger smile when he saw the handbag and the purse. He stuffed the small purse into the handbag without checking either, then went upstairs to look for more cash and stuff.

His smile almost hurt when he found the jar in Jack's shoe with a role of $100 bills that Jack had used to buy hookers. And when he found Jill's "mad" money

in her secret diary behind the fake part of her top drawer he just couldn't help it any more. He started laughing.

Now, anyone who really knew Benny knew he never laughed. In fact most of Benny's friends had never even seen him smile.

But on this night he laughed all the way to the alley, swinging the black handbag like it was a toy.

He laughed and even whistled a little down the three blocks to the back of the Safeway grocery store where he was going to go through the purses and toss them in the dumpster. Every time he thought how much money he had found and how easy it had been, he laughed. He reached the dumpster and opened the handbag. He was set for the next two weeks. He didn't have to worry about a thing.

Well, maybe not.

Seven

KEN THE POSTAL WORKER was still mad and still at large. And at the moment he was sitting beside the trash compactor behind the Safeway grocery store wondering who he should kill next and who he was the maddest at.

He saw Benny walk up with the woman's handbag in his hand and open it over the dumpster, smiling and whistling. And because Benny was smiling so much Ken just shot him.

Benny, being a big strong boy, dropped the handbag into the dumpster and staggered back.

Ken followed him, pointing the gun at him.

Benny choked a little because the bullet had hit his left chest, nicking his lung.

But somehow he had enough strength to keep moving away from Ken.

And Ken just followed him.

Right down the side of the grocery store.

Right across the parking lot.

And right into the street, where a cop named Roger spotted what was going on and yelled for Ken to halt.

Ken shot Benny again, twice.

Then turned to shoot Roger. But Roger had been around a few blocks before and he fired first, twice, killing Ken.

While all this was going on out front of the grocery store, it was trash day around back. The huge dump truck manned by Jerry and Tom picked up the dumpster and emptied it, handbag and all.

Then, since the Safeway was their last stop for the day, they headed for the city landfill not realizing what they carried, or the fact that they had run over blood stains from a recent shooting. To them it just looked like V-Eight Juice.

They dumped their load in the smelly landfill and left.

Henry's penis was buried under a truck-load of garbage and bad lettuce. It would never find its way to Henry now.

Well, maybe not.

Eight

THE NEXT DAY a plow driven by ex-lawyer Carl pushed the pile of garbage into a hole to move it out of the way so more trucks could dump their loads. Carl, like the justice system he used to play with, was mostly blind, so he never paid much attention to what he pushed around with the plow. He just moved it around to make room.

Constance Poe, a perky blonde with a good attitude and a lousy ex-husband, drove her Datsun pickup up to the edge of the landfill. She had been planning to move and was searching for a small house to buy and make her very own. But while she was searching, she figured she might as well be cleaning out her apartment and she had filled her Datsun pickup with junk to take to the dump.

She opened the door, wrinkled her nose at the sour smell, and choked back down the instant breakfast she had had earlier. She hated the smell of garbage.

Her big black dog Shep jumped out and went sniffing around. He, on the other hand, loved it.

"You be careful," Constance yelled to Shep as she started tossing the junk from the back of her truck onto the other piles of garbage.

Carl's moving of the pile had exposed the handbag and opened it slightly.

Shep sniffed the bag, stuck his nose inside, and pulled out Henry's penis.

Then with one gulp he ate it and went back to sniffing around.

Now it was certain that Henry's penis would never find its way back to Henry, and to the burial it deserved. Henry was clearly going into the afterlife dickless.

Well, maybe not.

Nine

CONSTANCE finished unloading the truck, got Shep back inside, and headed for home. All the way she left the windows down to clear out the smell of the dump and Shep rode with his head sticking out the window, his tongue hanging out, drool splattering the passenger door.

At home she cleaned up by taking a long shower and tossing her clothes into the washer.

Then she spent a quiet evening listening to the news and all the awful things that had been going on around the city that day.

The next morning, she called her real estate agent, who said there was this great little house where the owner had just died and did she want to take a look? It wasn't officially for sale yet, but the agent knew the attorney who was handling the place and knew it was going to be on the market real soon. Constance could get a real jump on it.

Constance said it sounded a little disrespectful to the dead, but sure, why not, really. The owner of the house was dead, after all, so who would really care. She and Shep piled into the truck and met the agent, Selma, at the house.

The house was a mess, with unwashed dishes and lots of garbage everywhere.

But to Constance it had possibilities.

And the back yard had this great hot tub. Blue, with great tile around it.

The agent didn't mention that the previous owner had died in the hot tub. What Constance didn't know, wouldn't hurt her, the agent figured.

And while they talked about the house, Shep took a shit.

Right beside the hot tub.

Henry's penis had come home.

When Constance moved in she planted a wonderful flower garden beside the hot tub and one flower grew even bigger than all the rest, right from the spot where Shep had shit.

Well, maybe not.

~

DEAN WESLEY SMITH

THE LIFE AND TIMES OF BUFFALO JIMMY

Chapters 31-33

What Came Before...

Nineteen-year-old Boston native Jimmy Gray had been traveling with his parents and older brother, Luke, headed west to find a new home and new riches. Before even reaching Independence, they were attacked and robbed by Jake Benson and his gang. Jimmy's parents were killed, his brother wounded.

In one of the wildest towns in all of American history, Jimmy Gray, a sheltered, educated son of a banker from Boston suddenly finds himself very, very much alone. But then through some luck, he finds other young men about his age and down on their luck who might be able to help him.

Together, the five of them head west after Benson. They end up hunting buffalo as he always dreamed of doing, but then they are hit with a massive flash flood and Jimmy is left alone, his friends more than likely dead. Luckily, they all meet up again and are all safe. So they continue west, knowing that Benson is just ahead of them.

Suddenly they come upon Benson and his men killing a farm family. They manage to get one of the men separated from the others, but in a fall he accidently dies. So they scatter to meet up later at a camp. They managed that but found a survivor of the killings. So one of them had to go back with the kid while the others followed Benson.

They caught him once again terrorizing a small wagon train and managed to scare him and his men off. But then they had to cross the forty-mile desert. And right from the start, things started off deadly. Then, in the middle of the worst part of the desert, they find a wagon train, horses stolen, water gone, only women and children left to die by Benson.

But what can they do? If they try to take them along, everyone will die. They decide they can't leave them and take them, barely making it to the river. Barely.

THE LIFE AND TIMES
OF BUFFALO JIMMY

Part Thirty-One
BACK INTO THE DESERT

JIMMY CRESTED OVER the ridge and looked at the deadly Forty Mile Desert. Its rolling sand seemed to stretch forever.

He and his friends had just made it across that desert. They had barely escaped the intense heat and lack of water the first time across.

Now they were riding back into the desert.

Again.

Into the very good chance of death.

Again.

Jimmy felt more scared this time than the first time. Now he knew the dangers, and how close, very close, the desert had come to killing them all.

He remembered the intense agony of every step, the thirst, the feeling of fighting off losing consciousness and just falling into the hot sand.

Yet, within five days of beating the desert the first time, they were going to challenge it yet again.

This kind of stupidity he was sure was what got people killed in the west. And up until now, all of them working together had been pretty smart. At least, they had survived.

Challenging the Forty Mile Desert a second time wasn't smart.

After making it across the desert the first time, they had stayed for three days on the banks of the Truckee River, camping with the women and children they had rescued.

Jimmy had not minded camping next to the river that long since the time allowed him to get to know Caroline a little better. She was his age and her father had been killed in a river crossing in the Wyoming Territory. It was just Caroline, her mother, and her little sister trying to make it to a homestead they had in California. She had no idea what they were going to do next, now that their wagon and all their supplies were lost.

For the first two evenings, Jimmy and the rest his friends had talked among themselves about giving up on their chase of the killer, Benson, and helping the women over the mountains and into California.

But by the third day, they still hadn't decided what to do.

Jimmy's goal was to track Benson and stop him, get the deed to the gold mine back, and make Benson pay somehow for killing his parents and all the other people he and his men had killed along the trail from Independence.

But at the same time, Jimmy couldn't leave these women and children alone without food or supplies.

Joshua had suggested they just stay near the river helping the women recover for a few days and an answer might present itself, but then when pushed, he had just smiled and not said any more. He clearly had a plan, but he wasn't sharing that plan with any of the rest of them, no matter how much they pushed him.

His only comment was simply to say, "It's too crazy to talk about yet."

None of them had seemed to mind the stay at the river either. The shade of the big cottonwood trees and the coolness of the river kept them all comfortable.

Truitt spent his time learning how to cook new recipes from the women, which was just fine by Jimmy and the rest.

Zach struck up a friendship with a girl named Sandra, and they spent a couple evenings walking along the river bank after dinner.

Longfeather was just happy that they were giving the horses time to rest. His passion was clearly those seven horses, and keeping them well.

Josh spent most of his time with his feet dangling in the cool water writing in his notebook, and every time he finished a story, C.J got to be the first to read it.

It was also Josh and C.J. who had enough reading to know some basic medical help for the older women who were slow to recover. Long as well had a few wilderness cures, as he called them, and they all three learned from one of the older women on how to treat sun-burned skin.

So it was three days well spent, as far as Jimmy was concerned, even though they might be getting farther and farther behind Benson.

On the evening of the third day, the wagon company that they had helped save from Benson back on Goose Creek arrived at the river, all of them splashing into the water just as Jimmy had done when they had arrived, even though it turned out they hadn't run out of water.

They were all happy to see each other again, and over dinner that night, Jimmy told the new arrivals what Benson had done to the women's wagon company.

They were all shocked, and said they had wondered what happened when they saw the men and wagons.

It was at that point that Josh told everyone about his plan. With enough men and horses, Josh thought they could go back and rescue the women's wagons.

Jimmy hated the idea.

Hated it.

Period.

The last thing he wanted was to go back into that desert.

Ever.

If he had to go back east to get his brother, Luke, he would go north and go on the Oregon Trail before crossing that desert again. As far as he was concerned, Josh had lost his mind.

But the men from the second wagon company who had just come off the desert thought it was possible, and the light in Caroline's eyes at the thought of having her family things back made Jimmy keep his mouth shut and think about it.

After talking with Long about the horses, and thinking about it for a few hours, he knew Josh was right.

He still hated the idea.

But he knew it was a good idea to go back into the desert for this reason.

Two days later, after the new wagon company's horses were well rested and watered, they set Josh's plan in motion.

Zach, Long, and Jimmy took all seven of their horses and loaded them with water bags and canteens and enough food and salty jerky to last for a day.

Three men from the new wagon company also went with them with nine of their horses. The plan that Josh had come up with would save five of the women's wagons.

If it worked.

They left after dinner, as the air was starting to cool near the river.

As Jimmy rode out of camp with a wave from Caroline, his only hope was to see her and the river again.

Part Thirty-Two
THE PLAN

THE RIDE BACK to the women's wagons, on rested horses, actually didn't take very long. Going through the first time, it had seemed to take forever to walk from the wagons to the river. But being fresh, rested, and on horseback, riding fast and after dark, the ride back out into the desert took less than four hours.

That eased Jimmy' worries a little, but not much.

They were back in the middle of the sand and there were still a bunch of things that could go wrong.

Very wrong.

When they reached the women's wagons, the sun was not even starting to color the morning sky, but the moon gave them more than enough light to work by.

They emptied the personal possessions of the women from two of the most damaged wagons into the five wagons that seemed to be in the best shape. They shifted some of the load around so that two of the wagons were much lighter than the other three. Two wagons had to be pulled through the sand with just two horses each. The heavier wagons would have four horses in harness.

They moved the men that Benson had killed, and the two dead women, and laid them out to one side of the two wagons they were leaving behind.

Then, with a few words from one of the older men, Jimmy and C.J and Zach covered the bodies with a little sand and put a makeshift cross near them. It was the best they could do for the dead in the little time they had dared spend.

Jimmy knew it was much more than most people who died on this desert got.

They didn't bother even covering the body of the dead killer. He wasn't worth their time as far as Jimmy was concerned. Jimmy was just glad that Benson only had one man left in his gang.

With everyone riding in the wagons, they headed back to the river before sunrise.

So far, the plan seemed to be going perfectly.

So far.

But the Forty Mile Desert was the most deadly stretch of trail that Jimmy could ever imagine. He wasn't about to go underestimating it now. Just being out on it again was crazy.

Zach drove one of the two light wagons with Jimmy riding along, since they were the two most inexperienced with wagons. Between the two of them, they managed to stay close to the wagon in front of them.

Long drove the other two-horse light wagon.

The men from the wagon company, with the experience of getting wagons all the way from Independence, drove the other three.

It got hot, very hot, sitting up on that wagon seat as the morning wore on and the sun climbed overhead.

Jimmy managed to keep his face in the shade of his hat and his hands and arms out of the sun as much as possible.

The sand kicked up by the horses pelted his skin like fine shot from a gun, and his eyes felt like they were coated in sandpaper.

Both he and Zach were constantly washing their eyes out.

The lead wagon driver drove the horses at a good pace and stopped every hour to rest them. Every hour they also rotated the horses between teams of two on the light wagons, and teams of four on the heavy wagons.

They all drank their fill of water, and gave the horses as much as they wanted as well. They had brought enough water with them to drink at that pace for a day. But if something happened to slow them down, they were going to have to cut back quickly.

Much to Jimmy' relief, nothing happened.

They crested over the rise above the river in just under ten hours, and were welcomed back into camp near the river with a wonderful dinner, just twenty-four hours from the time they had left.

The smile on Caroline's face that evening when she saw her family's things was worth the trip back into the desert for Jimmy. She had even kissed him on the cheek to thank him, and then she made sure that he promised to come by their new homestead outside of Sacramento.

It was a kiss that Jimmy would always remember, and a promise he planned on keeping.

Part Thirty-Three
BACK ON THE CHASE

THE NEXT DAY, Jimmy waved at Caroline one last time, and then he and his friends left the Truckee River and headed up into the hills for Virginia City. They still had to somehow find Benson again, and stop him from killing any more people.

And they had to get the gold mine deed from him.

The closer they had gotten to California and the gold fields of Northern Nevada and the Sierra Mountains, the more they had talked about finding gold and striking it rich. It was great campfire talk almost every night now.

As they crossed over the ridge outside of Virginia City, Jimmy wasn't sure what he had been expecting, but it sure wasn't the large booming town that faced them.

Virginia City seemed almost as large as Independence, and covered a wide hillside as well as stretching down into two valleys. There were mine tailings in giant piles in dozens of locations among the buildings, and there wasn't a tree to be seen anywhere near the town.

Dust from horses and wagons drifted over the town like smoke.

The place looked very hot, and very alive. Even from a mile out, they could hear the piano music from the saloons, and occasional gunshots echoed off the mountains behind the town.

"We need to find a place to camp," Jimmy said as they all sat on the ridge staring at the town.

"Most of the mining claims are down the valley to the south," Josh said.

"And right in the middle and under the city itself," C.J. said. "If we go west, beyond the town, and over those low ridges, we should find fresher water and a place to camp."

They talked for a minute about how they should go into town.

Long felt that it might be asking for trouble if he went right into town without first seeing how the residents of Virginia City treated Indians.

Jimmy didn't like that, but after Long insisted, he went along.

Long and Truitt turned west, leading the packhorse. The two of them would go around the large city, while Jimmy, Zach, C.J, and Josh rode into town. They would all meet near dusk a few miles outside of town on the Carson City wagon road that connected the two towns.

Twenty minutes later, the four of them rode into the center of Virginia City, Nevada, the most dangerous town that existed west of the Mississippi, looking for a deadly killer.

To be continued next issue…

USA *Today* Bestselling Writer

DEAN WESLEY SMITH

A
**Buckey the Space Pirate
Story**

CUCUMBER PARTY

At science fiction conventions, lots of very, very strange things happen. And considering that over the years, I've gone to hundreds and hundreds of conventions, I have my share of stories I would be glad to tell over a drink some evening.

Bucky the Space Pirate started life in a story called "The Sexual Voyage of the Starship Shirley" which ended up in OUI Magazine. *That story was about an event at a science fiction convention, just as this story.*

However, I want to be clear. I have never been on the Starship Shirley or been to a Cucumber Party. That's my story and I'm sticking to it.

CUCUMBER PARTY
A Buckey the Space Pirate Story

I WAS DRESSED in my Buckey the Space Pirate costume sitting in the hallway with about twenty other people in costumes, my back against the wall in front of room 1212, when she handed me the cucumber.

"Pass it on," she said in a husky whisper.

Then she winked at me. She had the edge of her eyes taped back and black cotton glued to her eyelids in typical alien-cat fashion. The wink made her look as if she was closing her eyes from a bad migraine.

"Hell, thanks a lot," I said.

"Hopefully, it will be myyyyyyyyyyyyyyyyy pleasure."

She tried to make the "my" sound like a purr, but it came out more like she was gargling.

Then, with one more migraine wink, she headed off down the hall with her tail with a big black fur ball on the end whacking people who sat along the walls.

"I can't believe it," my best friend Alex said. "You've been invited to a cucumber party."

I held the warm green cucumber up in front of me and studied it. I wasn't sure if I wanted to know where it had been or how it had gotten so warm.

"It is kind of hard to believe, isn't it?"

I'd heard of cucumber parties before. Hell, who hadn't? They were the latest "in" things at science fiction conventions.

The first time I'd heard of one had been two conventions ago at Biggerthanlife Con.

And at Biggerthanyours Con last week, there had been rumors that people were actually thrown out of the hotel for participating in one.

I stared at the cucumber in my hand. Now I was invited. Me, Buckey, a simple space pirate, at a cucumber party.

The very idea of it made my stomach churn and my mouth water from excitement.

And it was only Friday night. The convention was just getting going. This was going to be one damn good convention.

"Can I go with you?" Alex asked and reached to fondle the cucumber.

"Look, Alex. I don't—"

"It's Hoover," Alex said, demanding he be called by his costume character name. "And I don't see why I can't go."

I looked at the cucumber and then at Alex. He looked damn stupid in his Hoover, the Jovian Fur Merchant costume. He'd tacked two of his mother's old fur coats together and it smelled of mothballs something awful. No girl in her right mind would get within ten feet of him, let alone join him in a cucumber party.

But what the hell. This was a science fiction convention. Stranger things had happened. He just might get lucky.

"All right," I said. "You can come along."

Alex brightened right up and smiled a I'm-better-than-you smile at the guy dressed like Darth Vader sitting across the hall from him.

The guy just breathed a little louder.

"You got any idea how we can find the party?" I asked.

I twisted the cucumber in my hands. "There doesn't seem to be a room number here anywhere."

Alex's smile dropped into a frown as he thought about trying to find the party. In a hotel that had over fifteen hundred rooms, if you didn't know exactly where the party was, which wing, which floor, the only thing you were going to get was sore feet.

Alex shrugged, so I held the cucumber up for the other dozen people sitting along the hall to see. "Anybody know where the cucumbers are meeting tonight?"

All the people in the hall shook their heads and looked envious, except a young girl dressed as a flat-chested elf in green tights. "There's usually a map on the cucumber," she said. "At least that's how I found it last night."

All the envious faces immediately turned toward her like they were all on the same string.

I looked at her a little closer. She looked tired. For some reason, I took that to be a good sign.

Alex took the cucumber from my hand and studied it. "It doesn't seem to be a map of the hotel," he said.

"Of course not," the tit-less elf said and looked disgusted. "If you can't figure it out, then you don't belong at the party."

I took the cucumber back from Alex and held it up so I could see it better in the hall light. Its skin looked more like the back of a frog. Sure enough, there etched in very fine lines was a map. Or what someone might call a map. It didn't look so much like a map as a spider web made by a half-drunk spider.

Definitely not a map of the hotel.

Great. Just great.

"Come on, Alex," I said and stood. "I know where it's at."

I set off down the hall in the direction of the elevators, letting Alex scramble after me. I really didn't know where I was going, but I sure didn't want to sit there and admit it to that no-tit elf and the heavy-breathing Vader.

We took the cucumber back to my room and took turns trying to figure out what the map meant.

After an hour, I had a headache and no real good ideas.

Alex figured the entire map was a code for a room number in some alien language. Maybe Martian sanskrit or Antarian stone drawing.

Fat lot of good that was going to do us, but Alex figured it was either room 816, 927, or 1419. He wouldn't tell me how he came up with those numbers and I couldn't come up with any at all, even holding the map up to the mirror.

I figured if he was wrong, we could always just walk the halls until we saw someone else with a cucumber.

Room 816 did end up having a party going on in it. A two-person party in which the man, dressed like a Doc Smith Lensman, Lens and all, didn't like being disturbed.

No one was home in 927.

At room 1419, Alex knocked. "This is the place," he said. "I'm sure of it."

I just shrugged. If it wasn't, I was going to need to go to the convention suite to get a Diet Coke and some cookies. No wonder the no-tit elf looked tired. She couldn't find the party either.

A woman with only a towel wrapped around her answered the door. She had green eyes, light blonde hair, and toenails painted bright orange. I was in love at first sight.

I pushed Alex aside, took off my white-plumed hat and bowed slightly. "Excuse us. We seem to be having some—"

"Midge," the girl said, shouting back into the room. "They're here."

"Well, let them in," a voice said from deep in the room.

The girl stepped back and let the door swing completely open.

Alex nudged me. "I told you," he whispered, and pushed past me into the room, leaving a smelly trail of mothballs.

"Oh, God," Alex said as he got past the bathroom door and entered the main part of the room.

Orange Toenails motioned for me to come in, then closed the door behind me and let her towel drop to the floor.

I don't think I've ever had my mouth go so dry so suddenly as it did at that moment. I felt like the planet Dune had been transported to the top of my tongue.

Orange Toenails had a great body. Medium sized boobs with huge brown nipples, light colored pubic hair, and a small butterfly tattoo on the inside of her right thigh.

I must have kept walking as I stared at Orange Toenails, because I bumped into Alex who had stopped just inside the room.

"Oh God," he said, again.

I glanced around to see what he was oh-Goding, even though I didn't want to stop staring at the beautiful body of Orange Toenails and that butterfly tattoo in a place I so wanted to explore.

On the closest of the room's two beds was a long-haired woman without a stitch of clothes on. She had her legs slightly apart and I could see just a hint of Never-Never Land no one was going to have to fly to get to.

"Oh God," I think I said.

Or Alex said it. I wasn't really sure at that point.

All I know is that my Buckey the Space Pirate costume was suddenly very tight in the crotch.

Buckey Junior wanted out real bad.

"You're still dressed," the woman on the bed said softly to Alex and me.

Somehow I closed my mouth.

Swallowing was out of the question.

Orange Toenails reached for my belt and started pulling me toward the empty bed. "I'm so honored," she said. "I've never made it with a famous writer."

I started unbuttoning my shirt as she worked on my pants.

Out of the corner of my eye I could see that Alex already had his mother's fur coats off and was climbing on the bed.

"I've read all your books," Orange Toenails said.

She helped me out of my pants.

Buckey Junior saluted her.

Right about then I certainly didn't want to ask her just what the hell she was talking about. Hell, I hadn't written any books. I could barely write a term paper when I was in school.

But if this was the reception a writer got at these conventions, I was sure willing to learn.

She had my pants off and pulled me down on the bed with her. "Just let me do all the work," she said, kissing her way past my neck and heading down my chest.

I think Buckey Junior waved hello as she got closer.

"My pleasure," I think I managed to choke out.

On the other bed Alex was saying "Oh God."

Over and over again as the long-haired woman rode his mid section like she was riding a bull in a rodeo.

I hoped for Alex's sake she didn't have spurs.

Miss Orange Toenails swung her leg up over my chest and took Buckey Junior in her mouth at the very same moment she sat down on my face.

She tasted of a cross between hotel soap and Oolong tea.

I loved it.

I might become a tea fan after this.

She ran Buckey Junior in and out of her mouth with vacuum pump skill while at the same time moving her hips on my nose in a slight circular fashion.

I tried to concentrate on letting my tongue explore the strange new world and kept thinking about going for a five-year mission, but with the excitement of the moment, Buckey Junior just couldn't hold on.

She worked at draining him dry, not letting one drop escape while I managed to find a world I had never explored with my tongue.

Then she turned suddenly around and cuddled against my chest, pressing her boobs against my side and pressing her crotch into my leg.

"That was really nice," she said.

"Yeah," I said, trying to stop the light fixture on the room from spinning. "That it was."

On the other bed, Alex let out one last "OH GOD" that they must have heard two floors up, the long-haired women threw her head back, and from my viewpoint, they crossed the line in a photo finish.

"Would you sign one of your books for me?" Orange Toenails said, looking up at me and fluttering her big green eyes.

"I'd love to," I said, "but—"

"Oh, nifty-keen," she said.

Nifty-keen? Who said that?

She jumped from the bed, grabbed a stack of books off the dresser, and set them down beside me on the bed.

But if this was the reception a writer got at these conventions, I was sure willing to learn.

Then she sat down cross-legged on the bed facing me. I could see all of the strange new world my nose and tongue had just explored.

Buckey Junior twitched enviously at the sight.

I forced myself to look down at the pile of books.

The top one was "The Edge of Planet Ten" by Aaron Frost, Jr.

Oh, no, she thought I was Aaron Frost. That's why the reception. Alex had been wrong. This wasn't the cucumber party. Now what the hell were we going to do?

I flipped the book over. On the back jacket was a picture of Aaron Frost.

I had to admit, he did look a little like me. Only a bunch older.

What happened if he suddenly knocked at the door? Obviously he had been expected. That meant he was still on the way. The best thing Alex and I could do was hit the road quick.

"Look," I said, clearing my throat. "Since you both have been so nice to me, I've got a very special limited edition of this very book in my room."

I tapped the top book.

"You do?" Alex asked. He didn't understand what had happened, so I tried to give him the sign to be quiet.

"I do," I said. "And after this wonderful reception, I would love for both of you to have a copy, personally autographed by me. We'll just run and get those and be right back."

"You'd do that for us?" she asked, looking almost in tears.

"After this wonderful encounter, which I shall always remember, it's the least I can do. Then I can sign all of these and maybe we can have a rematch. All right?"

That sounded so weak, I couldn't believe she'd fall for it.

"Ohhhh…. That would be great," Orange Toenails said.

She bought it. I couldn't believe it.

"Why don't I just stay right here?" Alex said.

"No," I said. "I need you with me. To help me find the books. We'll be right back, ladies." I jumped off the bed, grabbed Alex's clothes, tossed them at him, then started putting mine back on. All the time I kept expecting to hear a knock at the door and it would be the real Aaron Frost with BIG friends.

I would be dead for messing with his date for the night. I had this clear image in my mind of me being stoned by Aaron Frost fans with his books as I ran naked down the hall.

"You promise you'll come back?" Orange Toenails asked.

I looked at where she was sitting cross-legged on the bed with all her charms exposed.

"Of course," I lied.

Buckey Junior wanted me to take the chance and just stay for a second round. But somehow, I got my pants back on, Buckey Junior tucked safely away, and Alex out the door.

"What the hell was that all about?" Alex asked as I halfway pushed him down the hall toward the elevators.

"Wrong party," I said.

"You mean that wasn't a cucumber party?"

"Nope," I said. "They thought I was Aaron Frost."

"The Aaron Frost?" Alex asked, then shook his head. "No wonder. The lady I was with said she had a story she wanted me to give to you to read. Lucky I didn't ask her why like I was going to."

In the elevator, I punched the floor number for the bar. Damn, I needed a drink.

Two floors down, two large-chested women dressed in harem girl costumes got on. Both looked really, really nice.

Alex had grabbed the cucumber on the way out the door, so I handed it to the shortest of the two just before the bar floor.

"Room 410," I said, giving her the number of my room. "Midnight. Just the two of you."

She looked startled, then happy. "Thanks," she said and waved as I pulled Alex off the elevator before he could ask me what I was doing and spoil everything.

We'd be waiting for them with our own special cucumber party. And if this worked, I'd bring my own cucumbers to the next convention.

Maybe a dozen of them.

Maps and all.

Coming Next Month...

More Buckey

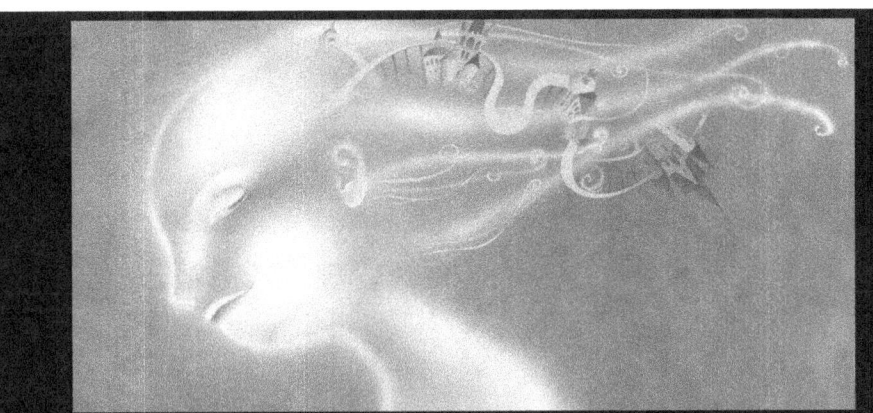

Poems by DEAN WESLEY SMITH

Patience

Patience comes
To those who wait

and wait
and wait
and wait
and wait.

But not necessarily
lunch, good service,
or sex.

And not necessarily
in that order.

DEAN WESLEY SMITH

THE ADVENTURES OF HAWK

Chapters 31-33

What Came Before…

Nineteen-year-old Danny Hawk, his uncle, and his best friend Craig, were in Cairo to look for his missing father. Danny had witnessed the death of his only contact in Cairo, Professor Davis, because the professor had Danny's father's journals.

Danny knows that the men who had killed the professor were now after him and the journals. Danny finds the journals and they decide to keep searching for Danny's father and try to rescue him. Along the way, Danny and Craig find some help from a street kid named Bud and twins from South Africa who had worked with Danny's father. They managed to escape the men chasing them over and over.

They finally decided to head out of Cairo. Beyond the headwaters of the Amazon, in the Republic of Congo, after a few more close calls, they hire a guide to take them into the jungle in search of a lost ancient city. Even into the jungle on the Trail of Elephants, they are followed. Then Danny barely escapes death when he falls through a floor in an old temple. The rest rescue him, but when they reach the bottom the men following them throw down the rope and trap them under the ancient city. But what they find next is amazing. An ancient council chamber.

And they find the fourth Hydra Journal entry.

HYDRA JOURNAL ENTRIES FOUND SO FAR
--The water flows uphill.
--The birth of a snake, the path of elephants.
--Under the teaming masses, the river becomes clear, the path muddy.
--From the highest city, power flows to the many.

So they head for South Africa where Ed and Ernie are captured.

THE ADVENTURES OF HAWK

CHAPTER THIRTY-ONE

October 2, 1970
Cape Town, South Africa.

THE POLICEMAN RAISED his gun at Danny Hawk and shouted, "Halt!"
Danny stopped, then carefully turned and raised his hands above his head.
Never, in all his life, had he been so scared. He had been in a lot of rough situations over the years, and even more since his father had gone missing. But having some large man in a brown uniform point a gun at him was the most frightening.

Around him, the huge three-story tall warehouses of the Cape Town shipping docks felt like huge child's blocks. They blocked the sun from getting down into the narrow alleys between the buildings, but didn't block the heat. And right now, Danny had sweat running down the side of his face. He wasn't sure if it was from the heat, or from the fear.

Probably both.

If this plan didn't work, he just might spend a lot of years in a South African prison. And right now, standing here with his hands in the air and a gun pointed at him, he wasn't sure about anything working, let alone getting his friends, Ed and Ernie Ellis out of jail.

For all Danny knew, he might be shot where he stood.

"What are you doing down here?" the man asked, not lowering his gun. The guy was huge, carried the gun like it was a toy, and looked mean, with a pock-marked face and balding head.

"Looking for my dad, sir," Danny said, in his best British accent, following the cover story he and Craig and Bud decided on earlier. "He was supposed to be down here. His name is Carl Conley. My name's Carl Conley Junior."

Carl Conley was a name Bud had seen on an office sign near the dock headquarters. The guy either ran this entire docking facility, or was near the top. Danny had no idea if he had a son or not, but he had to take a chance that the guard wouldn't know if the big boss did or not. After all, this was a huge docking facility.

The guard lowered his gun instantly and smiled a sickly smile. "Oh, sorry. I was just doing my job, you understand."

Danny took a deep breath and lowered his hands, going on with the plan he, Bud, and Craig had come up with. "No harm done."

Bud had said that the best plan was the boldest plan. Right now, Danny didn't feel so bold. He just hoped the guard didn't notice that his hands were shaking.

The guard put his gun away and then smiled again, stepping closer to Danny. "Any idea where your father was supposed to be?"

"His secretary said he was going to be at a jail," Danny said, continuing his bold lie. "I think she called it a holding area. She said it was in one of the warehouse buildings. He was coming down to see two prisoners. She gave me directions to the building, but I got lost."

Danny knew he was only one building over from the jail holding the twins.

"You didn't miss it by much, young man," the guard said, laughing. "And don't worry on getting lost. I still get turned around in this maze of buildings and I've worked here for years. Follow me."

He led the way between the two buildings and then to a door in the side of one warehouse that Danny had seen the twins taken through.

Danny walked in ahead of the guard, trying to act like he belonged where he was.

The small jail was just like an office, with two desks, a few extra guns on the wall, and a refrigerator tucked down a small hall behind one desk. The small window was barred and dirty.

The place was stuffy, hot, and smelled stale and sickly, like some drunk had thrown up the night before.

Another large guard sat behind the desk to the right, and through a barred window in a door behind him, Danny could see one of the twins in a windowless cell.

"Conley is on his way down here," the guard who had escorted Danny into the room said to his friend. "This is his kid."

The guard behind the desk stared at Danny, clearly not believing his story.

Danny knew he looked rough and his clothes were slightly dirty from being in the jungle, even though they had managed to wash most of their things while on the ship from Kenya. Danny knew he didn't look like an executive's son.

"Thought Conley's kid was younger," the guard behind the desk said, frowning and looking at Danny carefully.

This was going too badly. This guy knew Conley.

"I grew up," Danny said, shrugging.

Suddenly, a loud crash filled the room. Something large had slammed against the building near the jail door.

Danny ducked for cover behind the desk, still playing his part, acting like he was suddenly afraid. Both guards headed for the door, guns drawn. Danny just hoped Craig and Bud stayed out of sight.

As the two guards reached the door, another crash echoed from the next building.

"Stay here, kid," one guard said to Danny over his shoulder as they went outside on the run.

The moment they went through the door, leaving it wide open, Danny headed for the twins. The keys to the jail cell were hanging on a peg beside the door and Danny grabbed them.

Outside, one of the guards swore in pain.

Clearly, Craig and Bud were distracting them. Danny wasn't sure he wanted to know how. Bud had said to trust him, the guards would be distracted.

Danny sprinted into the darker cell area.

Ed was in the cell to the right, Ernie to the left. The place smelled of urine and vomit.

"Danny!" Ed said, moving to the bars.

"What are you doing here?" Ernie said.

Both looked shocked and very happy.

"Jailbreak," Danny said. "But if we don't move fast, I'm going to join you."

And Danny didn't like the sounds of that at all.

CHAPTER THIRTY-TWO

October 2, 1970
Cape Town, South Africa.

THERE WAS ANOTHER crash outside as Danny fumbled with the keys. He finally found the right one after what seemed like an eternity and opened Ed's cell door.

From outside, one of the guards again swore in pain. Then there was a gunshot.

The sound froze all three of them.

Danny's stomach twisted even tighter at the thought of Bud or Craig getting shot.

"Hurry," Ernie said as Danny again fumbled with the keys.

"I'll get our passports and papers," Ed said, sprinting for the front office. "I saw where the guard put them."

More swearing and shouting from outside, this time a little more distant.

Danny finally got Ernie's door open and the two of them ran for the outer office.

Ed slammed a drawer and held up his and Ernie's papers with a smile. "Got them, and the money those two took from us as well."

At the outer door, Danny had the twins stop and he went out first, looking around. No sign of either of the guards. Just sounds of swearing from the other side of the warehouse across the paved alleyway.

There was no one else in sight.

The plan had been for Craig and Bud to lead the two men to the west, while Danny and the twins went in the opposite direction. They were to meet up somewhere near dock 86-B.

Danny indicated that the twins should follow him, then at a run, they turned left and went down the side of the warehouse, then a quick left again around a corner of the building. They ran for the length of two large warehouses, turned right, ran the length of yet another, and then turned left again.

Danny was really starting to get winded in the heat when Ed said, "In here."

They ducked into an area between two buildings that was stacked with dozens of piles of wooden pallets.

"You are amazing!" Ed said breathlessly to Danny, patting him on the back.

"We thought we were dead for sure," Ernie said.

"We all might be if we don't find a good hiding place," Danny said, looking both ways down the narrow alley between the warehouses. He was sweating so hard, it was stinging his eyes. They all were going to need something to drink pretty soon as well in this heat.

"We can't keep going together," Ed said.

Ernie nodded. "This is still South Africa. Whites and blacks can't be together doing anything, unless the white is in charge."

Danny just shook his head. He understood the reality of that, but he sure hated it. Just as he hated it when people treated him differently, or put him down for his Native American heritage.

"Where are we meeting Bud and Craig?" Ernie asked.

"And how are we getting out of here?"

Danny explained that he had booked them all passage on a British freighter heading for South America, but it didn't leave port until 7 A.M. October 4th.

"That's two nights and a day away," Ernie said.

Danny nodded. He knew that, and was very worried about that as well. This was a very busy port, well-patrolled. Now that the twins had escaped, everyone would be looking for all of them. Hiding was going to be a real problem. Just getting to dock 86-B was going to be a problem. That was a good mile from where they were.

"Here," Ed said, pointing back at the pile of wooden pallets.

Danny, at first, couldn't figure out what Ed meant. This alley clearly wasn't a good hiding place. And it was far too close to those two guards back there.

Then Ed moved to a dolly with four wheels and a handle. There were three of them parked in the alley.

"Pallet movers," Ernie said to his twin brother. "Great thinking."

"Want to clue me in?" Danny asked.

"Watch," Ed said. He grabbed one machine, quickly moved it around like he had handled the thing before. It had two long blades on the front that slipped in under the bottom pallet. With a few quick pumps on a handle, Ed picked up a six foot high stack of empty pallets.

Ernie quickly did the same thing, rolling the pallets out into the open.

"Now, you walk behind us, pretending like you're in charge of what we're doing," Ed said. "We're taking these to dock 86-B."

"You're the boss," Ernie said firmly to Danny, looking him right in the eye. "Remember that and act that way."

"I hate this," Danny said.

Ed smiled. "This is what our parents fought against and died trying to stop."

"Some day it will stop," Ernie said. "But for now, we live with it and get out of this country."

"Can't be fast enough for me," Danny said.

CHAPTER THIRTY-THREE

October 2, 1970
Cape Town, South Africa.

THE THREE OF them got a few odd looks from other workers along the way, but no one stopped them. Danny hated acting like he was in charge of his two friends just because of their skin color. But he tried to, and Ernie and Ed pulled the stacks of pallets carefully, slumping over like they were used to the hard work.

Finally, as they neared the dock where the British freighter would hopefully take

them out of this country, Danny heard Bud whisper from a nearby open warehouse door.

"Here."

Danny and the twins glanced over to where Bud was in the dark shadows just inside a warehouse door.

The twins quickly moved the wooden pallets over into an area that held other pallets, then the three of them went inside.

It took a minute for Danny's eyes to adjust. But it soon became clear that the warehouse was stacked completely full of huge crates. Some of the stacks reached clear to the tall ceiling three stories overhead.

The air inside was cooler than outside, but not by much.

The huge shipping doors of the warehouse were closed, and the only light came from a few high, dirty windows.

"Is Craig all right?" Danny asked as Bud led them deeper into the darkness of the warehouse.

"We heard shots," Ernie said.

"Just fine," Craig said, stepping out of the shadows. "Can't say that I like getting shot at by the police, though."

Danny patted his best friend on the shoulder. "Just think of all the stories we can tell the girls when we get home."

Craig laughed. "Yeah, like they're going to believe us."

Danny laughed as well, very happy to see his best friend alive and well.

"I've found a great place to hide," Bud said.

He led them, single-file, deeper into the giant stacks of crates until they were near the middle-back of the warehouse. Then Bud pointed upward.

"We climb up there and hide on top, or inside those top crates, depending on what's in them. We'll know if workers start moving these things. We'll have

time to make a break for it. And guards aren't going to climb every stack in here looking for us."

"Perfect," Ed said, nodding.

"But we're going to need water," Ernie said.

Danny looked up at the tall stacks of wooden crates towering over them. He wasn't real excited about spending the next two nights in here, but at this point, they had no choice.

Or at least none that he could think of.

"The next warehouse over has an office in it," Bud said, pointing to the west wall. "I'm sure we can find water there at night, after everyone's gone. And we have enough food to last us until we get on board the ship."

With that, Bud turned and started up the side of the stack of huge wooden crates like he was climbing the side of a rock mountain. It was as if Bud had spent most of his life climbing wooden crates. He didn't miss a step or a handhold and before Danny realized it, Bud went over the top and disappeared.

A moment later he poked his head back over the edge. "Easy. Everyone take their own stack. But these things are so close together, if we have to, we can run across the top of them."

Danny remembered the terror he had felt jumping from one roof to another over an alley in Cairo. He really didn't like the idea of jumping from crate to crate over a thirty-foot drop.

But so far, in looking for his father, he'd done a lot of things he didn't think he'd ever do. He just hoped crate-jumping ahead of guards with guns wouldn't turn out to be one of them.

Continued in the next issue…

Now Available
from all your favorite booksellers
in trade paper and electronic editions.

USA *Today* Bestselling Writer

DEAN WESLEY SMITH

Some Marriages
are Shorter
Than Others

MARRIAGE IN SIX FLOORS

I wrote this story back in what I call my "horror period" of writing. In fact, back in that period I was nominated for a Stoker Award a few times, which is the award given out by the Horror Writers of America.

I tend to think of this story as a mystery story instead. But honestly, it never occurred to me to send it to one of the mystery magazines.

So finally, it sees the light of day. Yet another side of my writing.

MARRIAGE IN SIX FLOORS

FIRST FLOOR

THE DRUG WEARS OFF.

Jagger Swayne finds himself standing, arms tied behind him. Cold metal presses hard against the full length of his back.

His jaw aches. Something soft and wet jams his mouth open, wraps around his head, and pulls the skin of his face painfully tight.

His vision slowly clears.

He stands in a small, dark, cement room that smells of mold and damp. It is a cold smell.

A smell that holds years of sameness.

The room is very small, not much larger than a closet.

His head misses the metal ceiling by less than a foot.

Through the dark, he can see lines of shadows on the opposite wall.

He pushes the haze of drug back into the corners behind his eyes and tries to think.

Jagger Swayne.

His name is Jagger Swayne. He is from Chicago.

Can he be crazy if he can remember his name?

No? Clearly, he is here.

But how?

Susan.

Dinner in their honeymoon suite.

The wine.

Her smile as she watched him drink.

Damn it, Susan.

If this is a stupid trick, it is not funny.

Six Months Earlier...

Jagger punched his finger against the up button and turned to the woman named Susan he had just met in a bar about four blocks away.

She had long blonde hair she kept pulled back and a classic face that had only a little make-up on it because she didn't need it. She wore a light sweater that clearly showed the lace bra under it.

She was exceptional, seemed to have many secrets, and yet laughed easily. She was from out east, she said, and was only visiting the beach for a short time.

He was on business in Seattle, and had never even been to this beach resort town or old hotel before, but he was growing to like it by the moment.

He flat couldn't believe she had agreed to go with him tonight from the bar. His friends back in Chicago would say she was out of his class and too old for him, and after his money and more than likely they would be right. But at the moment he didn't care.

She leaned against a section of the brass that decorated the old Lost Cove Hotel's main lobby. As he watched, her gaze drifted around the plush lobby, drinking in the lushness of the turn-of-the-century setting. Her mouth was slightly open, her eyes shining. He could tell that she liked what she saw.

He liked what he saw as well, staring at her.

"They say that every room has a view of the beach," he said.

"And I suppose you've had girls in all of them," she said, laughing, knowing that he had never been here before.

"Of course not," he said with mock seriousness. "The top floor is the honeymoon suite."

She tried to tickle him, but the door to the old elevator slid back with a clank and he ducked inside. She ran her hands along the marbled mirrors and polished brass of the interior as she followed.

"This is really something."

"It is, isn't it?" he said, staring at her wonderful body and smiling face and long blonde hair.

He pushed the first floor button on the brass control panel and then leaned back against the side wall, staring at her. "Beautiful."

"They say this takes forever to just go one floor."

She moved across the small space and into his arms as the door slid closed. "So we might as well make the best of it."

He laughed as the lift jerked upward and locked them together.

SECOND FLOOR

FAINT VOICES OVERHEAD wake him.

Jagger Swayne tries to yell, but the gag chokes off all but a low moaning sound.

He tries to kick, but his legs are tied as tightly as his hands.

Rope winds across his chest and over and under his shoulders, keeping him so tight against the metal bar that he cannot slide down into a sitting position.

Another rope cuts into the skin around his neck and hangs down in front of him like a long necktie.

That rope ends in a large pile at his feet.

A loud jolt echoes in the small room. Movement.

He tips his head back tight against the rope.

The ceiling is moving slowly upward. Light cuts bright gashes across the dark from cracks in the opposite wall. What were streaks of shadow suddenly become greasy black cables.

He is under an elevator.

The bar pressed into his back vibrates. It is the rail the elevator moves on.

In front of him, a thick rope hangs down the center of the shaft. It is tied to the bottom of the elevator and now slowly uncoils from the pile at his feet like a slow-moving snake.

The other end of that snake is his necktie-rope.

He frantically kicks and struggles against his bonds as the elevator slowly moves upward. The slight whisper of the rope uncoiling covers his muffled screams.

Finally, a loud thump echoes down the shaft as the old lift engine on the roof shuts down. The elevator stops at the second floor.

He tries to take a deep breath against the gag to calm his adrenalin-pumped heart.

Footsteps sound above.

Then faint laughter.

Susan will pay for this.

Four Months Earlier…

"You really like this old hotel, don't you?" Susan asked as she pushed the up button of the old elevator. The door eased open slowly as if the hotel was yawning.

Jagger set the suitcases down against the back of the elevator and leaned against the brass and mirrored wall. "It feels like home to me." He shrugged. "There's just something here."

He didn't want to say that what was special was her. And he loved meeting her here.

"Ever think you'd like to spend the rest of your life here?" she asked. "Never go back to Chicago?"

Again, he shrugged, staring at her. "If possible, I probably would. I don't know why. I just like it."

She pushed the button for the second floor.

The door slid closed and the elevator bumped slowly into motion. "Maybe it's this old elevator," she said, and then kissed him.

As the elevator plodded, he came up for air. "That has a lot to do with it."

She laughed, and they kissed for the rest of the ride.

THIRD FLOOR

MORE VOICES.

Sweat stings his left eye. He blinks the sweat back.

The elevator rises.

The rope snakes off the pile.

The elevator passes the second floor. He doesn't know how much rope is in the pile. He fights against the bonds that hold him tight against the rail. He doesn't know if he is loosening the ropes or not. He cannot feel his fingers.

A loud thud.

The rope stops.

He stops fighting, shakes the sweat from his forehead and looks up. The elevator is at the third floor.

The old hotel only has six floors. There didn't seem to be enough rope left in the pile for three more floors. How often did they rent out the top floor honeymoon suite? Maybe he will get loose or someone will find him before then.

How much time did he have left?

An hour?

A day?

The elevator clicks and starts down, blocking out more and more of the light as it comes.

This had been their honeymoon night.

But how can she do this?

Putting him here seems even beyond her.

What had he done?

He had hoped to be a good husband.

She didn't give him a chance.

He glances up.

The elevator descends on him like the sky falling in a nightmarish dream. He tries to duck, but the ropes will not let him. The elevator rattles to a stop a foot over his head.

Damn Susan.

She will never get away with this.

Never.

He hears the door slide open. Footsteps shake the cage above him.

He calls out against the gag and tries to shake his body to make noise. The ropes cut deeper into his flesh.

The door closes.

Again, silence fills the tiny concrete darkness and lets the smell of the mold and the damp crawl back over his face.

Three Months Earlier…

"What do you really like about me?" Jagger asked as they waited arm in arm for the elevator to get to their third floor suite in the old ornate hotel. "My money or my smile?"

"Your money, of course," Susan said, and then giggled in her little-girl giggle. "But you kiss real nice, too."

"What happens when I get old and have dentures? What will you do then? You can't kiss my money."

She leaned against him as the elevator bumped past the second floor. "Don't worry," she said, smiling at him. "I'll find some part of you to kiss."

She always could say exactly the right thing.

FOURTH FLOOR

THE ELEVATOR STOPS and he stops screaming into his gag.

He closes his eyes and tries to swallow the thick taste of fear in his mouth. He doesn't dare throw up.

He would drown.

He takes slow measured breaths, then tips his head as far back as the noose will allow. Above him, the light comes into the shaft from the cracks around three doors. The rope sways in the center of the shaft like a pendulum marking the last moments of his life.

He stares up the nightmarish length and tries to think.

Why had Susan done this?

She had been rich in her own right. She didn't need his money. Or at least he thought she didn't need it. Even though a friend had warned him, he hadn't signed a prenuptial. If he disappeared, she would have all his money.

And none of his friends even knew he came out here. And Susan had always insisted on paying for the room.

She clearly has planned this for as long as she has known him.

But how can she expect to get away with this?

His body will be found.

He studies the ground around his feet. It's dirt. And has clearly been dug up a few times in the past.

Are there others under that dirt?

Is that where other husbands are buried?

Other lovers? How many are down there?

He pushes that thought away.

How did she get him down here?

Did she have help?

Of course she did. More than likely she has a real lover as sick as she is.

A partner.

The man with the sly smile and dark eyes behind the front counter of the hotel desk.

Of course.

She always demanded they meet at this hotel, always.

The elevator bangs against the track as it starts down. He feels it through his arms and his back.

The ache in his jaw is intense.

He tries twisting his head back and forth to loosen the gag. His skin burns against the rope. Blood drips into his collar and runs down on his shoulder.

At his feet, the pile of rope grows.

One Month Earlier…

"You sure you want to be Mrs. Jagger Swayne?" he asked Susan as he set the suitcases down against the back of the elevator. He could not believe that in a moment of passion last time he had proposed to her and she had accepted.

She smiled and rubbed against him like a cat against a leg. "It would feel really nice."

"You know," he said, as he punched the fourth floor number. "The sixth floor honeymoon suite is the only floor in this hotel we haven't stayed on."

"Good," she said. "On our wedding night, we'll break it in right."

The door slid closed.

And he liked the sound of that.

FIFTH FLOOR

THE ELEVATOR STARTS up and he comes alive.

He measures time with the rope going up and down.

Up and down.

His remaining life is measured by the soft whispers of the snake coiling and uncoiling at his feet.

Stretching up, then back.

Up.

Down.

Up.

Down.

Up.

He screams through his gag.

She has everything planned. She has pictures of him walking along the rock cliffs above the beach, she has pictures of him taking out a fishing boat.

He will vanish and no one will know what happened to him.

And she will take his money.

One Week Earlier...

"Did you hear something?" Jagger asked, breaking away from Susan's embrace as the elevator started up.

"Just my mind thinking how much I love you and how much I can't wait for next week."

"I had this feeling," he said. "Cold. Really cold. And a muffled scream." He tilted his head, trying to listen over the noise of the old lift.

"Suddenly getting afraid of marriage?" Susan asked, using her lower-lip pout.

"No, of course not. I must have just imagined whatever it was. You know how I am when I get excited." He winked at her.

She giggled.

SIXTH FLOOR

FOOTSTEPS ABOVE and he knows.

This is it.

This is the time.

It has been almost two days.

Maybe Susan had figured wrong. He watches calmly as the elevator pulls the rope past the second floor and keeps going.

He can almost hear her voice above him.

This is the one and there is not enough rope.

He spits Susan's name against the gag. He hopes she chokes on his money.

No one stops the elevator.

No one will.

He did this to himself. He hadn't been able to see the real Susan, all he had been interested in was the sex.

It seemed she had money. He never figured out where she got the money from. Now he knew.

He hadn't paid attention to all the signs, the rush to get married, the desire to always come to this old hotel, to not meet his family and friends until later, to surprise them later, she had said.

They would be surprised when he vanished without a trace and so did all his money.

He closes his eyes and waits.

At his feet, the rope slowly uncoils and measures him with a soft brushing sound.

Above Him...

"We should open the champagne while we're still in the elevator," Susan said to her new husband, Benson Stevens. "When we get to the room, I have other things in mind."

She rubbed against him, more turned on and excited than he had seen her before.

They had dated for about six months in Portland up until he asked her to marry him. She had said she needed some time to think about it and had vanished back to Seattle for a number of months, calling him to tell him she still loved him, but she couldn't decide.

Last night she had called and said if he wanted to marry her, they needed to do it tomorrow before she got cold feet. The wedding had been quick and easy in Reno, then they had flown back on his private jet to what she called "Their hotel," for the honeymoon.

He loved the old hotel. They had visited it often. The place always seemed to turn Susan on even more than usual.

Benson picked up the bottle from where she had set it under the control panel with its lit number six. "Always thinking," he said.

"I try," she said, rubbing against him.

He had the outside wrapping and the wire off the bottle by the time they passed the fifth floor. He planned to pop the cork just as they reached the top.

Two feet short, the elevator slowed.

Then it paused, as if it didn't want to go all the way.

He could hear the elevator engine straining.

Straining.

Until Finally...

The elevator jerks upward.

The newlyweds bump together.

The cork pops off the bottle with a much louder sound than he had expected.

Benson holds the bottle up while the champagne bubbles out and drips on the carpet leaving a dark, round stain.

Susan damn near climbs all over him, kissing him with more passion than he could ever imagine a woman having.

The door to the sixth floor slides open, exposing the huge honeymoon suite with its plush red carpet, red hearts on the walls, and huge tub next to a stone fireplace. A massive four-poster bed dominates the center of the room.

He pushes the hold button and pours the champagne.

First her glass, then his.

"A toast to us," he says.

"And marriage," she says, giving him that smile that he both loved and that scared him just a little.

Their glasses click lightly together.

He doesn't notice she doesn't drink a bit of the champagne as she lures him into the big room before the drug takes effect.

~

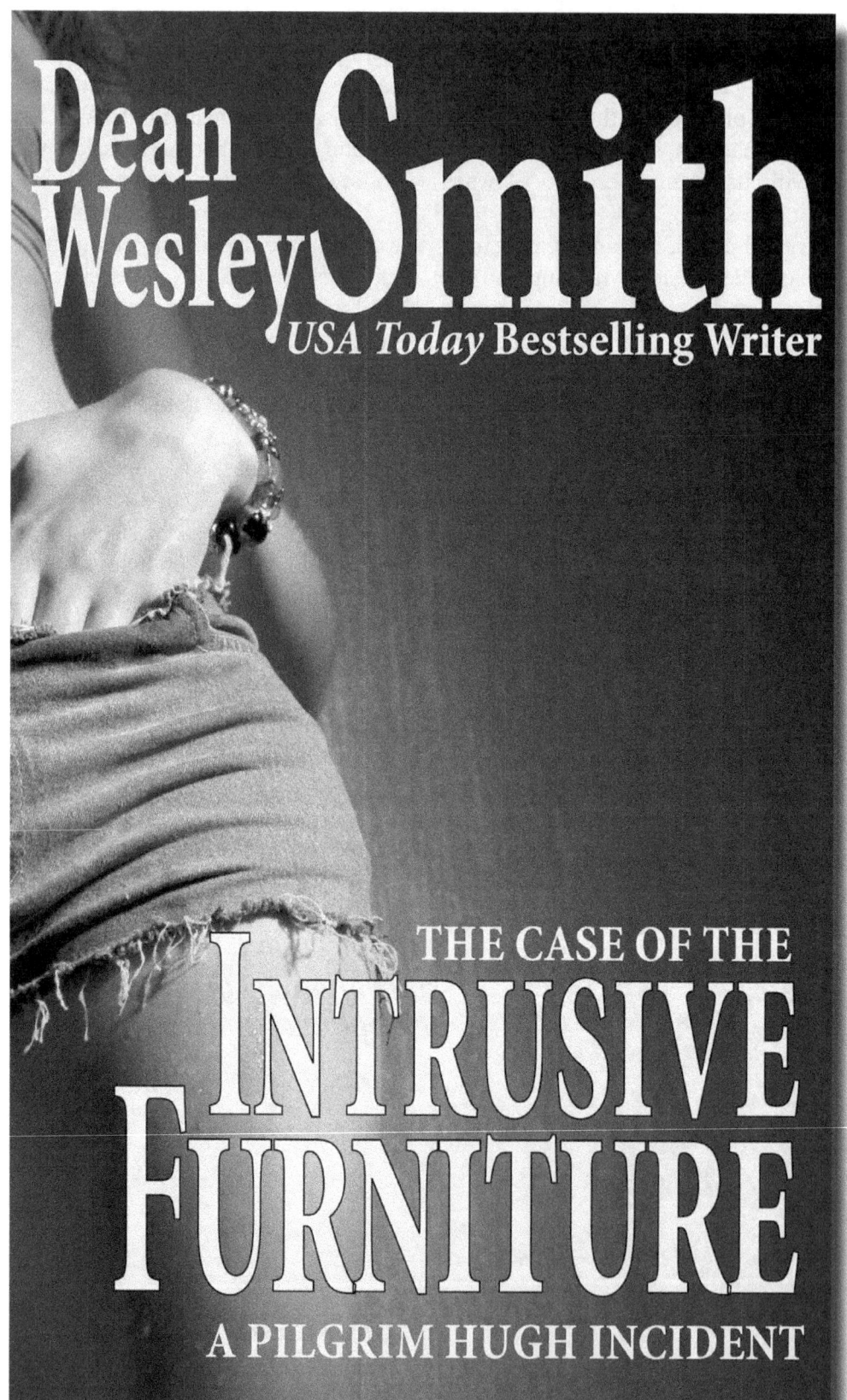

Dean Wesley Smith

USA Today Bestselling Writer

THE CASE OF THE

INTRUSIVE
FURNITURE

A PILGRIM HUGH INCIDENT

Pilgrim Hugh solved some odd cases before, but an old, smelly couch sitting in the middle of a beautiful lawn seems to have full-blown strange written all over it.

With his friend and beautiful assistant, Carrie, he must figure out why the couch ended up there and what the woman living in the perfect home hid (besides a bad facelift and a heart of stone).

A very cold case on a very hot day.

THE CASE OF THE INTRUSIVE FURNITURE
A Pilgrim Hugh Incident

ONE

PILGRIM HUGH HADN'T seen a piece of furniture so ugly since the night his first wife had attended an auction in a barn and mistaken chicken droppings for a French designer signature on a chaise lounge.

Just like that chaise lounge, the standard American couch in front of him on the perfectly mowed, perfectly green lawn could not have been given away, let alone sold. The once tan cloth had faded to a pale, dirty white and one of the three cushions had a very large dark spot on it that looked to be the remains of a cola stain from a distant time in the past. Even the stain had faded.

And he hoped it was cola. Safer to just think it was and move on.

The couch looked long, like a full adult could stretch out and not touch either end, but damned if he was going to test that. What had started as a decorative wood trim on both arms and across the front of the couch was now scarred and dirty and the cloth on both arms had worn through to the threads.

The entire thing smelled musty and of long storage. He had spent many hours through the years, especially while in college and law school, on couches he was sure looked and smelled far worse. Only difference was those couches were in dark rooms, not sitting in bright sunshine in the middle of a freshly mowed suburban lawn.

He nodded to the poor cop named Dennis, a young kid with freckles on his nose, who had been unlucky enough to answer this call. Dennis stood in the shade of a nearby small poplar tree as Pilgrim walked around the couch, studying it, but finding nothing more than an old couch.

It was the kind of couch you see sitting beside a road with a "free" sign on it and no one takes it for a month and the rain ends up soaking it and the city finally has to haul it away and try to find the owners who dumped it to pay the costs.

Over the last few years as a freelance private detective and lawyer, Pilgrim had gotten some strange calls, but this call on a rogue couch had to rank right up there on the strange meter.

After he'd gotten out of law school at the ripe old age of twenty-four, he had gone to work in corporate law and had managed to last in the law firm through the two years of his first marriage before becoming bored with both. Then his grandmother, a woman he barely knew, died and left him more money than even he could imagine or try to spend. He had become free to do what he wanted.

So after a year of drinking and traveling around the world and another even shorter marriage, which got boring faster than corporate law, he went back to school to become a private detective.

Most of the training was not like the books about private detectives he loved to read. In fact most of what he had done was learn how to track someone by computer and look up financial records, which was flat dull.

Finally, out of desperation to do something interesting, he set up his own law and private detective firm, hired a couple of associate lawyers to handle the boring stuff, and offered his services for free to the different city police departments around the Portland metropolitan area.

Hugh and Associates was born, the strangest law firm to ever have plush offices in a downtown Portland high-rise.

A few old corporate clients paid very well and kept a growing staff of associates busy and the police forces started to take him up on his offer to look for free into strange and odd cases that no one else wanted to deal with.

Now, at the age of thirty-eight, he had been working to solve weird crimes and find missing people for almost a decade. And not once in those ten years had he been bored. Even now, staring at an old couch.

This couch was so out of place as to be funny in the middle of a well-kept lawn in the Portland, Oregon, suburb of Hillsboro. The three-story home seemed perfectly kept and no doubt a gardener did the yard. Pilgrim imagined the house inside to be as perfect as the lawn. More than likely the owners pretended to be just as well-kept, at least on the surface. This area was known for its pretend rich. He didn't want to think about the size of the mortgage on this house.

He shuddered at the thought of how close he had come to this lifestyle with his first wife, Karen. This would have been her perfect home. And he would have spent more time in Henry's Sports Bar than in it if he had stayed married to her.

Two

THE SUN BEAT on the old piece of furniture, making it smell even worse if that was possible. Clearly something musty and rotten was inside it as well. More than likely a number of dead mice.

Pilgrim stepped back onto the sidewalk and clicked his earpiece to talk to his driver. "Carrie, a couple Diets for me and the officer if you wouldn't mind."

"Shit," she said in his ear. "Too damn hot to go out there."

Pilgrim smiled as he watched her climb out from behind the wheel to bring him and the officer a couple of Diet Cokes. They both had figured this was going to be a quick stop.

She was right, it was hot. Portland didn't have too many really hot days, but today was promising to be one of the record-setters. The sun and warm June day was making him regret wearing a black Henry's Bar tee shirt this morning. He should have gone with the white Next Gen tee shirt and Bermuda shorts instead of the Levis.

He loved being self-employed and rich and able to wear anything he damn well wanted any time he damn well wanted. Sometimes dressing like an over-aged college student helped him on cases. People tended to talk with him more when he wore a tee shirt than when he had on his three-piece court suit.

Carrie went to the back door of the limo and retrieved from the fridge a couple bottles of Diet Coke and then grabbed

another for herself. Today she had on blue short-shorts and a white tank top that left little to anyone's imagination of what was under it. Her short blonde hair framed her deep blue eyes and chiseled features perfectly. She never wore make-up and never seemed to comb her hair, yet she always looked perfectly put together.

She was a good six-feet tall, just an inch shorter than he was, and looked like she belonged on a runway modeling dresses and underwear, even at thirty-eight. She had been Pilgrim's best friend since high school in Bend, Oregon, and acted more like his partner than his driver at times.

She had helped him get through two wives and far too many girlfriends to count. And not once had they slept together. It just seemed wrong to him, like sleeping with his sister, if he had had a sister.

She felt the same way about him. Over the years she had managed to keep boyfriends to the sex-and-leave stage that she liked. Never married, Pilgrim doubted she ever would. Not her thing as she often said.

Carrie had only one more year of law school and she would be joining the law firm side of his business. She had spent eight years in the military after high school learning computer skills and other things that constantly surprised him. Then she had traveled the world for a few years. During that time he got letters and messages from her from just about every scary hell-hole on the planet. Now she was just finishing her law degree.

She didn't handle boredom any better than he did.

Until she passed the bar, she paid her way through school and for her Penthouse apartment by helping him with cases and being his limo driver when he needed one for clients or for police cases.

For some reason he really, really liked showing up at a crime scene in a limo. It had become part of his image around town and he and Carrie had turned the limo into a major office and computer center on wheels. Tee shirts and a limo. Pure Northwest rich geek.

Pilgrim watched as Carrie headed up the sidewalk toward him. She had a sharp eye for details about a case that seemed right, but looked wrong. Just last week she had helped him solve a very obese woman's murder when both he and the police thought it nothing more than death by natural causes. The way the woman had fallen in the kitchen was just wrong to Carrie's mind and she led Pilgrim to discover the dead woman had a boyfriend who wanted her coin collection and thought murdering his girlfriend for the money was a good idea.

Why Chief Benson from the Hillsboro police had called Pilgrim on this "couch case" was beyond him. More than likely it was just something he didn't want to waste manpower on on a hot day and figured Pilgrim could find a way to make the problem just go away with some legal language. For Benson and the city, Pilgrim was free.

More than likely the guy in this house had donated a decent amount of money in the last election and had Benson's direct phone line.

It didn't matter to Pilgrim. He owed Benson many favors from over the years, so handling something like a misplaced couch on a lawn of a political supporter was the least he could do for him.

Pilgrim took the Diet Coke from Carrie, rubbed the cold bottle against his forehead, then opened it and stepped back to just stare at the intruding piece of furniture. More than likely this was just a bad joke of some sort being played on the family.

The plastic and wood wrapping that had brought the couch to its present location had been tossed to one side leaving the old couch sitting like a bad nightmare on the mowed grass.

Someone had paid a lot of money to have this old couch delivered here. Why?

The shipping instructions were with the wrapping so he went and retrieved them as Carrie came back from giving Officer Dennis his drink. More than likely, with what Carrie was wearing, her visit just heated the poor officer up more than the Diet Coke would cool him down.

The plastic wrap the couch had come in was very strange. Part of the plastic was clearly very, very old and had just cracked and fallen apart when removed, while another layer over the top was new, more than likely put on by the moving company. Clearly this couch had been sealed in that original old plastic for a very long time.

"So figured out *The Case of the Intrusive Furniture* yet?" Carrie asked, as he came back with the shipping instructions. "This is one for the strange disclosures file."

"Not a clue," Pilgrim said, shaking his head at Carrie. She really loved to name all their cases like mysteries from a 1940's serial radio program and planned on putting some of them into a book she called "Strange Disclosures."

There was nothing on the delivery instructions but the house address for delivery, instructions to open the plastic wrapping and just leave the couch on the lawn, and a greeting from a man named Thomas.

Pilgrim read the note on the shipping label aloud. "You liked this so much, I figured you should have it now that I am dead."

"Wow, that's cold," Carrie said, shaking her head. "You think that's blood on the cushion?"

"I'm hoping not," Pilgrim said, but after the note he was becoming less sure of his cola-spill theory.

He handed the shipping label to Carrie. "Get on the phone and talk to the shipping company. Get an address and name of where this came from and any information you can find on this Thomas guy, even if you have to threaten a subpoena."

She nodded, looking at the label in her hands. "You talking to the homeowners?"

"You got it in one," he said. "Feed me any information you might dig up along the way. Get a couple people at the office helping on this as well."

"Got it," she said and turned for the limo as he headed past the couch for the house.

Three

AS HE RANG the bell to the McMansion, he realized he more than likely should have gotten a sports coat from the limo. Someone in a home like this would give him more information if he looked like an investigator instead of an overgrown and aging college student.

"Too late now," he said to himself as inside he heard someone's steps coming toward the door over a hard surface.

A woman who looked to be in her late fifties opened up the door and a frown managed to cross over her face even with all the plastic surgery holding her skin in place. She had short brown hair done perfectly around her face. She wore a white blouse with a black lace garment under it that looked far too hot for the day. A cool blast of air-conditioning caught Pilgrim in the face as she glanced at him, then at Officer Dennis standing under the tree.

At one point this woman had been very beautiful. Fighting to keep that beauty had not gone well for her.

"Yes?"

"My name is Pilgrim Hugh," he said, handing her his card that said "Hugh Investigations" on it and nothing about him being an attorney. "Chief Benson of the Hillsboro Police sent me to look into the issue with the couch. Can I talk with you for a moment?"

She nodded and indicated by stepping back that he should enter enough for her to close the door to the heat. But she didn't offer to take him anywhere but the stone entryway. And she didn't introduce herself.

"Her name is Alice Bluehaven," Carrie said in his ear. *"Wife of Dan, mother of two grown kids both in college out of the city."*

Pilgrim glanced around as Carrie fed him the information. He had been right about the house. It looked perfectly maintained and impossible to live in. More like a home taken right out of a picture in a magazine. Sterile and angry-feeling. Just as the woman in front of him felt.

"I wish my husband had never called the police about this," Mrs. Bluehaven said, clearly upset. "It should just be hauled to the dump."

"What can you tell me about that couch?" Pilgrim asked.

"It belonged to me and my first husband, Thomas Williams. We lived in Chicago when we split up in 1984."

Pilgrim was surprised at that information. He expected her to not know a thing about the old furniture on her lawn.

"Married to Thomas Williams in 1981, divorced in early 1985," Carrie said.

"I don't want to press charges against Thomas for doing such a thing. I just want it off my lawn."

"It says on the note that he's dead," Pilgrim said.

"Then the executor of his estate should be replaced for doing this. That is just embarrassing to have sitting out there and I plan on having it removed as soon as possible."

Pilgrim was stunned. The woman was colder than her house. She had just been told her first husband was dead and hadn't even flinched or cared in the slightest. Even though Pilgrim and his two wives were divorced, he still liked them and would be very upset to learn that anything had happened to either of them.

Whatever heart this woman had once possessed had clearly been removed with the plastic surgery to her face.

And honestly, Pilgrim was starting to like this Thomas guy. He must have known what his ex-wife was like, that she wanted everything to look and appear perfect, and knew how to torture her perfectly after his death.

"Before I can allow you to have the couch removed," Pilgrim said, "I'm going to need more history."

"Why would you need that?" she asked, her cold blue eyes almost emitting sparks.

"Your husband filed a complaint and thus this is technically a crime scene," Pilgrim said, lying, or actually just stretching the truth some. "To clear the scene I need background about the couch and your former husband. Paperwork. Otherwise the couch will have to remain where it was delivered until we get to the bottom of all this, and that might take days without your help."

She looked appalled and shocked to her very cold core. The idea of that couch staying on her lawn all day and into the evening for her neighbors to see was clearly more than she could handle.

"What can I tell you?" she said, her voice cold and low and very mean. How this woman stayed married to any man was beyond Pilgrim.

"Why this particular couch? Why would your former husband keep it for decades?"

"I had an affair on it," she said, her voice level like she was telling him about the weather. "Thomas walked in and caught us. I grabbed my clothes and ran out the back door and never went back. I never talked to Thomas again."

"Oh," was all Pilgrim could say.

They stood there in silence for a moment. The house like a tomb around him. At that moment all he wanted to do was run for the limo and get out of the icebox this family called a home.

"Oh, wow, is more like it," Carrie said in Pilgrim's ear. *"This is really going into the Strange Disclosures file."*

"What happened after that?" Pilgrim asked Mrs. Bluehaven.

"I honestly don't know," she said. "I stayed with a girlfriend for a night, then flew back to Portland and stayed with my parents. Thomas filed for divorce and stayed in Chicago and I didn't fight it. As I said, I never saw him again after that day, so I would have no idea what happened next. Our marriage was clearly not doing well."

"Clearly," Pilgrim said.

She stiffened even more if that was possible, but said nothing.

"But even after all the years you still recognized the couch? How is that possible?"

"I would recognize that trash anywhere," she said, so disgusted she almost spit as she talked. "I wanted to get a new couch, but Thomas was so cheap he kept saying we couldn't afford it and that tattered old thing was perfectly fine. I refused to sit on the couch."

Pilgrim almost said, *But no problem screwing your boyfriend on it.* Luckily he stopped himself.

"One more question," he said, "then I think I can have Chief Benson close this case and remove the couch."

She nodded, clearly relieved.

"What was the name of your boyfriend?"

"I don't see how that would matter?"

Pilgrim smiled. "Just making sure all the details are in order is all."

"Craig Marshal," she said. "Craig S. Marshal. He was a graduate student at Northwestern. I never talked to him again, either."

"Got it, on it," Carrie said in his ear.

Pilgrim nodded and turned for the door. "This should be over shortly, Mrs. Bluehaven."

As he stepped back into the heat of the front yard and she closed the door solidly behind him, he had a hunch this was far from over.

And his little voice on cases was seldom wrong. Carrie just might be right. This might end up being one for the book.

Four

HE NODDED TO Officer Dennis and headed for the limo with only one more look at the couch as he went past. The heat actually felt good after being with that woman. She was one cold human.

But on the other hand, the couch was starting to get a real smell to it. And not a good one. He knew that smell anywhere. Something inside that couch was very, very dead. And the hot sun was not helping the issue at all.

As he climbed into the limo, Carrie was working the computer station on the right side. It had two large screens that dropped down from the ceiling and a full desk and keyboard that slid out from under the wet bar. Her fingers were flying over the keys while at the same time she was talking into a headset to someone, more than likely an assistant at the office.

From their car they could get just about any information they wanted. He had had it outfitted better than most offices. And both he and Carrie were damn good at hacking into places they shouldn't be hacking into. He just didn't allow them to do it without darned good reason.

After a moment she finished her conversation, thanked the person on the other end, and turned to him.

"The boyfriend vanished completely on October 4th, 1984," Carrie said, confirming what Pilgrim had feared had happened. "No sign of him was ever found."

"I have a pretty solid hunch where we are going to find him," Pilgrim said. "Did our couch-sender actually die?"

"Yes," she said. "Liver cancer from a lifetime of hard drinking. The couch was removed already wrapped as per instructions from the garage of the home and delivered as instructed. His death triggered the automatic pick-up and a neighbor let the movers into the garage. He has no executor. And no family as far as I can find. And not much of an estate beside the house."

"Great work," Pilgrim said, taking his phone and dialing the private line to Chief Benson.

"You think we have a body?"

"The smell in the sunshine around that couch isn't getting any better," he said.

"The husband killed the boyfriend?" Carrie asked.

Pilgrim could only shrug as Chief Benson came on the line, but for some reason Pilgrim doubted that the husband had done it. He had no proof either way, or even a body yet, actually, but there would be shortly. That sun and heat on the couch was going to make it perfectly clear very quickly where the body was located.

Pilgrim told the chief about his suspicions that the couch was an actual crime scene. "A very cold case crime scene," he said, "that is heating up by the moment."

"Why the hell do you always do this to me?" Benson asked.

"You keep calling me," Pilgrim said before the chief could hang up.

Carrie just shook her head at his lame joke.

Pilgrim had Carrie move the limo down the street and out of the way before the excitement started.

Ten minutes later the rest of the police started arriving. A number of police took up stations around the entire house and in the back yard while others taped off the area around the couch, then slowly worked to figure out exactly what was in the couch before hauling the entire thing to the crime lab.

While they waited, both he and Carrie worked the computers and phones digging up every bit of information they could about the woman and the lost lover and the man who had sent the couch.

Pilgrim actually talked with three of Thomas's friends and the bartender where Thomas liked to drink. Thomas only told the bartender that one day his wife had just left him for no reason. But all of his friends said that when she left he had never been the same. He hadn't seemed to get over it even after twenty-plus years.

That fit her story.

But something still just didn't feel right to Pilgrim.

At that moment Chief Benson knocked and opened the back door of the limo, crawling in with a sigh as the air-conditioning hit him. He was a stout man built like a longshoreman who always wore a tie and blue shirt and jacket. Even in the heat he hadn't taken off the jacket.

"I got to get the city to spring for one of these," Benson said, then laughed.

Carrie offered him a regular Pepsi in a can, the chief's favorite, then went back to her computer search.

"Thanks," he said, smiling at her. "Nice outfit."

"Keep your eyes up," she said without glancing at the chief.

Benson laughed and turned to Pilgrim. "So what more have you dug up?"

"I'm sure that the woman inside will want us to think that the sender of the couch murdered her boyfriend. She's setting us up for that. Take a listen."

He replayed his conversation with the woman for Benson.

"Wow, cold bitch," Benson said when it was finished.

"With enough plastic surgery," Pilgrim said, "to keep a doctor in new golf clubs for a long time."

"Figures," Benson said. "You ought to meet her husband. Short little guy who chases every skirt he sees. So what's bothering you, Pilgrim?"

"That obvious?" Pilgrim asked.

Carrie snorted and kept her attention on the screen in front of her.

"Like an open book," Benson said, taking more of his Pepsi.

"Well," Pilgrim said, "first off, if Thomas had killed the boyfriend and hid his body in a wrapped-up couch, he never would have kept the couch this long. Too much risk."

"True," Benson said. "It would have ended up in a landfill a long, long time ago. You just don't keep the evidence of a murder you committed in your own garage for decades."

"Exactly," Pilgrim said.

"But I have seen stranger things," Benson said.

So had Pilgrim, but he kept going. "When she let me in she refused to even look at the couch on the lawn. Like she knew what was in it."

"Not enough to even get a warrant, counselor," Benson said.

Pilgrim suddenly had another idea. "Carrie, can you find what day the woman of the house flew from Chicago to Portland back in 1984? She said she went within a day or so, but I'm betting she hung around."

Carrie nodded. "Good thinking."

A moment later she said, "Got it. She left three weeks after the boyfriend vanished. Not the next day as she claimed."

"So you think she killed the boyfriend and got the husband to help her cover it up?"

"More than likely," Pilgrim said. "You just have to get the motive out of

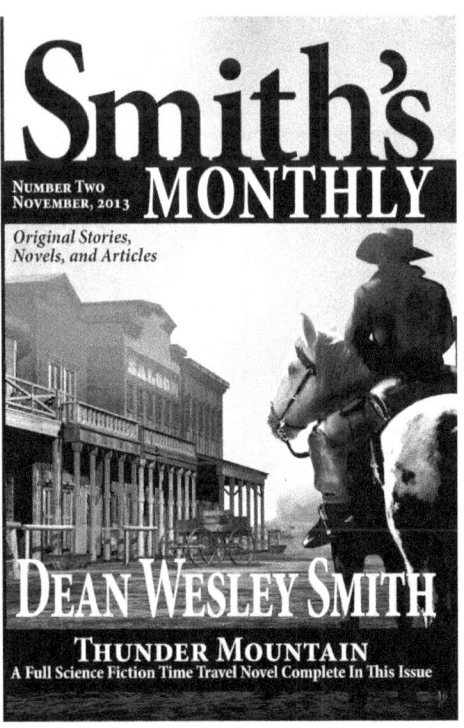

her. But either way she's involved with a murder. It would take two people to move that couch into a garage and wrap it with plastic."

"Looks like I had better go read someone her rights," Benson said, "before she sneaks out the back door."

"Take back-up," Pilgrim said as he climbed out of the limo with Benson.

"No worries there," Benson said, laughing.

"Well," Carrie said, climbing out of the limo to stand in the heat beside Pilgrim, "it seems like we solved *The Case if the Intrusive Furniture.*"

Pilgrim nodded. "I think the sun and heat helped."

"So what do you think actually happened?" Carrie asked.

"Not a clue," Pilgrim said, "and I'm not sure anyone will ever know all the details with the former husband dead. He protected her and himself for a lot of years, even though he wanted to pay her back once he was gone."

"You think he still loved her?"

"My guess is that he loved the idea of who she had been," Pilgrim said.

"You know," Carrie said, "it's not often we solve a cold case."

"Especially on such a hot day."

Carrie just moaned and Pilgrim smiled.

He glanced around at the neighbors now starting to gather and watch from a distance behind the crime scene tape. "At least now the world is going to know what was really inside that pretend shell she's kept up all these years. And that's going to hurt her more than jail time."

"So true," Carrie said.

Up around the old couch the crime techs had started to work at the back, but Pilgrim had no doubt what they would find.

The entire neighborhood would remember this smell.

Afternoon summer heat and a body that had been wrapped in plastic for twenty-eight years just did not mix well.

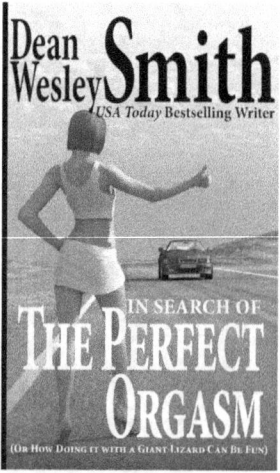

The Third Seeders Universe Novel
now available from all your favorite booksellers in trade paper and electronic.

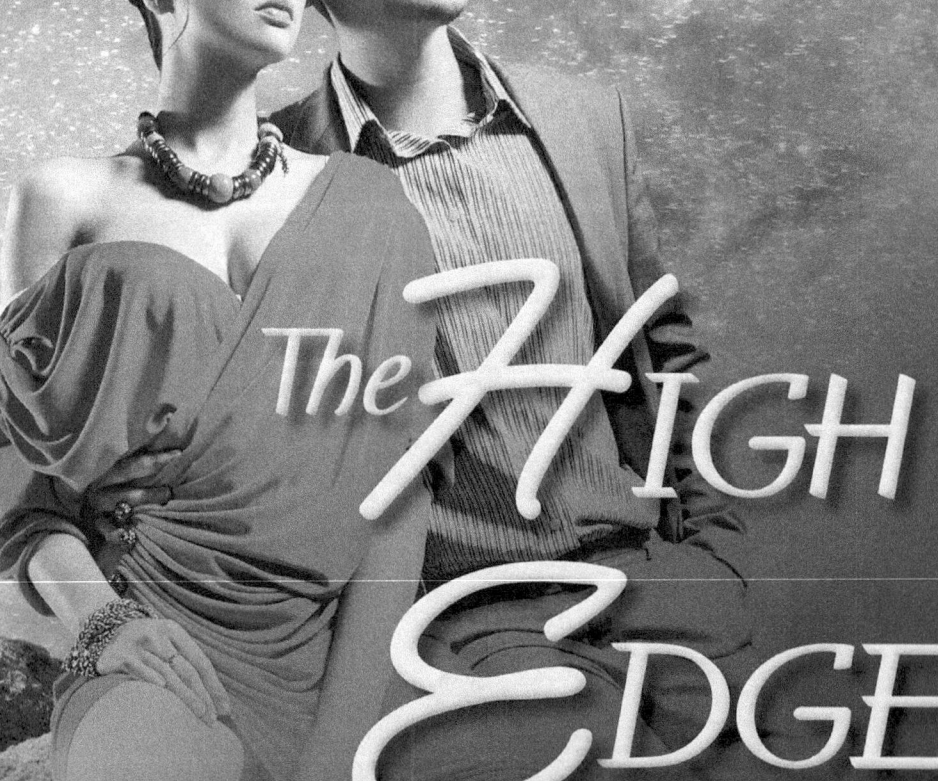

DEAN WESLEY SMITH

USA Today Bestselling Author

The High Edge

A SEEDERS UNIVERSE NOVEL

As with the four other books in the Seeders Universe so far, this fifth novel stands alone. All of the other novels also appeared in issues of this magazine and they are all out now in trade paper and electronic format.

In this book, Benny Slade lives in New York City. One moment the city around him (and everyone he knows) seems normal, the next moment, everyone dies.

Working to survive among the dead (and plan for a future) feels impossible, but Benny doesn't give up easily. Especially when he meets the woman of his dreams and she offers to help him and others survive. And then she offers him an even a bigger job, a job that could take him out into the stars.

THE HIGH EDGE
A Seeders Universe Novel

For Kris

THE DISASTER

Chapter One

SOMEHOW BENNY SLADE survived almost everyone else in the world dying.

One minute he went into his old steel vault that filled the back room at Benny's Personal Loans to get some cash for his next loan and when he came out, both Madge and Maggie, his two right hands, were laying face down on his newly installed brown carpet in the front office.

Madge, who looked more like his old mother used to look before she got hit by that cab, had fallen next to her always-neat and clean desk while Maggie, about two years younger than Benny's twenty-eight years, had sprawled in the middle of the floor, her short skirt riding up and showing him a little of those wonderful white panties of hers that he liked so much.

He had just come out of the vault with the two hundred and sixty in cash for Mrs. Tenny's loan. He dropped the money on his desk and just acted, not thinking.

First he called out to Maggie and kneeled beside her and checked her first. He couldn't find a pulse and she wasn't breathing.

Then he jumped over beside Madge. Same thing.

No pulse, no breathing.

Both were dead.

He sat back on his heels, still beside Madge.

He could feel that cold, hard feeling coming over him like it did when he had been in a firefight in Iraq.

He hadn't felt that in four long years.

He had hoped he would never feel it again.

With that cold, hard feeling, emotions got shoved back. He had needed that to happen in the gulf and it happened now.

He just stared at the two bodies in front of him.

What had happened? No one had come in or out because the bell hadn't rung on the door. And he had only been in the vault for less than thirty seconds.

It took him a good twenty seconds of staring at his two dead friends to figure out what was different, what was wrong besides two healthy women being dead.

He just kept kneeling there, staring until he finally saw it.

There was no blood.

Nothing.

They just lay face up, eyes wide open, completely dead.

"Move, Benny," he said out loud. That finally got himself into motion.

He stood and went to the phone and called 911, staring at the two women on the floor while he waited.

But no one answered.

With the phone to his ear, he went back and checked both of them again.

Very dead.

Very.

The phone was still ringing at the emergency center.

What had happened?

His first thought was gas attack, which got him moving even faster.

He took the phone and scrambled back into the vault.

He had left the vault door slightly open when he came out, so if it was some sort of terrorist gas attack, he was as good as dead as well.

Besides, he had stayed out in that front office for a good minute staring at his two friends and trying to call for help.

After fifteen seconds of standing in the dark working slowly to control his breathing, he got disgusted at himself.

"Come on, Benny, get it together. Do a little thinking. Use your damn head."

Madge had always complained he talked to himself too much, but Maggie thought it cute.

Maggie had thought anything he did cute, and he had thought she was cute.

They had flirted since the first day he hired her six months before. She was as sharp as they came and knew money and books and computers, even though she hadn't finished more than a year of high school. He was attracted but had managed to keep the relationship on only flirt level.

She had been fun, just not his type.

Even though he came across as the military type, he had two degrees from the City University of New York, including one in math. He liked women to be much, much smarter than Maggie. But she had still been fun to flirt with.

He went back out and stared at the two women on the floor. The phone to the emergency center was still ringing.

He hung it up and tried again.

It just kept ringing.

911 was slow at times in New York, but not that slow.

He didn't hang it up, just sat it on the desk and stared at Maggie there on the carpet for a moment. He was going to miss those white panties she flashed at him all day.

He was also going to miss her laugh and her smile and that wonderful blonde hair.

The coldness inside him whelmed upwards and he pushed those thoughts away. As his sergeant used to say, "Time to fight, time to think later if you survive the fight."

His sergeants over the years, all of them, had always been annoyed that he thought too much and didn't react quick enough when needed.

Clearly, this was some sort of strange fight he was in. He needed to get moving.

He turned away from Maggie and headed for the door.

At first, he opened the door slowly, not sure what to expect.

The moment the door cracked open, the wave of sound hit him like a hammer. He hadn't noticed that before because he always just blocked out any sounds from a New York street. Anyone living in the city needed that ability or otherwise go stark raving crazy.

He opened the door completely and stepped outside, going down the four small steps to the sidewalk.

The day was comfortable for an early summer day, with high overcast clouds that threatened rain. It wasn't very warm at all and wasn't supposed to turn hot for over a week. He hadn't been looking forward to the heat because he normally wore jeans, a long-sleeved shirt, and a sports coat over his shirt. Today he had on a tan shirt and dark-brown sports jacket.

But when the city turned into a giant sweat-box, he couldn't dress the way he liked and that just irked him.

He stood and took a deep breath of the cool afternoon air. Then he made himself really look at what was around him.

Up and down the street and on all the side streets hundreds and hundreds of car alarms and sirens were all going off at the same time.

Drivers were still in their cars, either slumped over, or head rolled to one side, held up by their seat belts. Cars had piled into intersections, had smashed into parked cars, or run up and against buildings.

Most car engines were still running, some racing as if their occupant still had a foot on the gas. Up Lexington Avenue he could see a fire starting to take hold of a building.

But what he didn't hear through all the noise were police and ambulance sirens.

And no one around him in the cars or on the sidewalk was moving.

No one.

This was some bad shit. Of that he had no doubt.

He quickly checked a couple of young girls on the sidewalk near his office front door to be sure they were dead. One had on a short blue skirt that had ridden up when she fell to show no underwear and he covered her up before checking her.

They were as gone as Madge and Maggie, eyes open.

He stared at their faces. They had not died in pain, that much he could tell.

No wonder no one had answered his call at the emergency number. From the looks of this, they were dead as well.

Then, up the street, he saw some movement as people came up out of the subway and sort of stopped and stared.

"So I'm not the only one," he said, feeling fantastically relieved.

He started toward the other people, then saw a couple of them panic and flee back down into the subway, followed by the others.

"Won't help," he shouted. But no one was going to hear anything over the noise of the car alarms and engines.

But they were doing exactly as he had done when he ran back into his old vault.

He glanced around at the buildings towering over the canyon of Lexington Ave. He couldn't see one window opening, or anyone even peaking out at all the noise.

And as far as he could see in both directions, everything was stopped and bodies covered the sidewalks.

He walked up to the corner of 54th,, carefully walking around the bodies. He looked both directions.

Same thing along the tree-lined street.

Everyone was dead, knocked down by some sort of giant killer in an instant.

From what he could tell, not a one knew what hit them. None of them looked shocked or panicked or were showing any fear at all.

Just normal expressions on very dead people.

"What happened?" he asked out loud, but the words barely made it to his own ears in the noise of alarms and running cars.

Who knew that the end of the world was going to be so damned loud.

"I need to find out how far this spreads," he said into the noise.

He could feel the panic he had learned to hold down when he was a kid in fights on the street and when in the Iraq war start to ease up into his gut. He hadn't felt that in many years. It wasn't the dead bodies that bothered him.

He had seen worse.

Much worse.

Dead bodies after the first few months in Iraq had stopped bothering him, at least on the surface. His counselor at the VA said he had a lot of buried anger and that the only way to get healthy was to let out some of the anger and tell the counselor what he had seen.

He didn't want to tell anyone, so he and counselor hadn't gotten too far in the last few years.

Death didn't really scare Benny, but there were dead bodies on his street, in his own business, and he was still alive.

Now that scared hell out of him.

He started to head back to lock up his vault, then laughed and looked around. Unless this was the second coming and everyone was going to suddenly spring back to life, locking up his money was the least of his worries.

But he went in and locked the vault anyway, tossing the money back inside that he had taken out to loan Mrs. Tenny for her grandkid's operation. More than likely Mrs. Tenny and her grandkid weren't going to be needing much of anything anymore.

Chapter Two

"WHAT A MESS," Gina Helm said, her voice soft, the shock she was feeling making her voice a whisper that didn't carry very far in the almost empty banquet room.

The hotel-like banquet room was large enough to hold five hundred people, but only she and ten others were in the room, staring at a large screen on the wall. Some were almost not breathing, a few were covering their mouths and crying silently.

The image panned over the area of the planet below where in ten days they would rescue the survivors from that last deadly pulse of electromagnetic energy from an exploding neighboring star. The images they were getting were from about five hundred feet in the air. The bodies of the dead littered the ground seemingly everywhere along the streets of one of the planet's largest cities.

In places, a few people moved among the bodies, but mostly all she could see was a sea of death.

How was a disaster like this even possible? The scope of it just stunned her.

She covered her mouth because she wanted to be sick, finally making herself turn away from the images of the dead for a moment. She strode for a few paces in the large, empty room, trying to clear her mind a little.

She was the tallest in the group at six foot, so her strides were long and covered distance across the hard, tan-carpeted floor. She had very short, black hair and she kept herself in perfect shape. Her steps were almost silent. She had on white tennis shoes, jeans, and a long-sleeved white blouse with the sleeves rolled up.

Her normal working clothes.

Today was not a normal working day.

She didn't like the feeling of being sick, of feeling helpless in any situation. She had learned to always be in top shape and never feel helpless on her home planet a few hundred years before, when as a young woman she had needed to become a survivor.

And she had.

Now she was here to try to help the survivors below.

She needed to pull herself together.

She turned and instead of looking at the large screen panning over the streets of death, she just stared out the huge wall of viewport that covered one side of the big room.

The beautiful planet drifted below, whites and blues swirling over the large oceans. It seemed so calm and peaceful and reminded her a lot of her home world. Looking at the planet through the wall-sized viewport, you could never tell the billions of humans who had thrived on that beautiful planet were now dead. Only a few million survivors remained.

She forced herself to take a few deep breaths to calm herself.

There were almost a thousand humans on this huge spaceship called *Star Conscious* that now orbited the planet. The crew and people like her on board were from over four hundred planets in three different galaxies near the Milky Way. Her home planet was in the Lesser Maganelic cluster of stars.

Everyone on this ship was a Seeder, part of an ancient organization of humans that seeded human culture on all Earth-like planets and then helped the human cultures survive and mature.

The planet below had been seeded.

She had been recruited to be a Seeder off her home world when she was twenty-five and now a few hundred years later she still looked the same, since once a person became a Seeder, all aging and disease was cured from the body.

The Milky Way had been completely seeded and the front edge of the Seeders had moved on to the Andromeda Galaxy and its surrounding satellite galaxies before she had become a Seeder. She had joined in with the social services branch and in two hundred years had been embedded on nine different worlds at differ-ent levels of development to help move the culture of that planet forward.

The planet below had been seeded in the third sector, so it was in the early space-age period of growth, one of the most dangerous periods for any culture. Only the humans on the planet below would now have to start over and build again.

She had no idea how long it would take them to get back to where they had been in development. Or if they ever would.

The mission below would be her tenth, and so far the most challenging. She had no idea how to help survivors just live and start to rebuild a civilization taken from them without warning in an instant.

The Seeders, even with all their ships and skills, hadn't been able to do anything to help rescue the billions of humans on the planet below from instant death, but they could rescue and help the survivors.

The *Star Conscious* had just arrived in orbit less than ten minutes ago, right after the first big death pulse. If that pulse would have been allowed to hit this ship, some inside would have died as well.

The Seeders who had been embedded on the planet below had escaped on one ship and would be returning to also help with the survivors.

Helping the survivors was why she was here. She and at least a thousand others covering the planet were going to help the survivors move forward as fast as possible, start to rebuild over the next twenty or thirty years.

But first they had to rescue as many as they could of the survivors from a second coming disaster. This planet wasn't going to be struck with just one electromagnetic deadly pulse, but two, the second one coming in just ten days.

Right now, from another more advanced part of the Milky Way Galaxy, ships were speeding here to try to pull off the planet the almost two million survivors and move them out of harm's way when the second huge pulse washed over the planet.

Then they would put everyone back to start the rebuilding process.

All of those ships from the Milky Way Sector One had Seeders embedded secretly in the crews. Every planet eventually discovered that they had been seeded at a distant time in their past, but the common knowledge was that the Seeders were long gone. In reality, Seeders were everywhere, secretly helping every culture advance and survive. Only the main wave of Seeder ships had moved on out of the Milky Way.

This ship was only one of four completely Seeder-run ships on this rescue mission.

She looked around. The large room looked like it could hold a banquet with a hundred tables. It had lights recessed in the ceiling and tan walls. In ten days this room would be full of at least three hundred survivors from below.

And thousands and thousands of other rooms like it on this ship and a thousand other ships would be full as well.

Staring out at the beautiful blue planet below, she just hoped enough of the other ships would make it in time to save every survivor from the second pulse.

Chapter Three

BENNY HEADED downtown along Lexington, stepping over and around the dead bodies on the sidewalks. He thought these sidewalks used to be crowded when people were alive. When the same people were sprawled all over the place, not moving, the sidewalks got even smaller.

A number of places he had had to walk out in the street to get around cars smashed up on the sidewalk. And in two places he had to actually climb over the hood of a car to even get up the street.

Most everyone had either their business clothes on, or summer clothes, so there was a lot of skin showing.

A lot of very dead skin.

He kept staring up at the buildings around him, looking for movement in any window.

Nothing.

Thank heavens the day hadn't turned hot.

Down a dozen blocks, he saw a few more people gathered near the entrance of the subway, looking terrified and very panicked, but at least this group had gotten over the desire to flee back into the tunnels. More than likely this was their second time to the surface.

Benny crossed the street, giving them a friendly wave as he went toward them. "Anyone have any idea what happened?"

All four of them, including a nice-looking young thing with blonde hair and a light blue backpack over her shoulder, shook their heads no.

One guy held up his cell phone. He looked to be about five years older than Benny and had more hair than any guy should ever wear in his mid-thirties. It was tied back into a ponytail.

"Phones are working, but no one is answering anything," he said. "Anywhere."

The guy stressed the word "anywhere."

The guy seemed to be the one who was in charge of the little group.

Besides the college-age girl, there were two boys about the same college age, all looking stunned. More than likely this had been some sort of field trip for a class and the older, long-haired guy was the professor.

The guy again stressed the word "anywhere," more than Benny wanted him to.

The other three nodded, all holding their cell phones as if they were lifelines. After walking a dozen blocks, Benny was starting to get the idea that no one was going to toss any of them a lifeline.

"Anyone try tuning in a radio?" Benny asked, something he kicked himself for not doing at once back at the office. He clearly wasn't thinking as well as he seemed to think he was.

That wasn't a good sign and he needed to make sure he was extra careful.

The guy nodded. "Nothing. The internet is still working, so is Facebook and Twitter, but not one new post from anyone, anywhere in the world, that we can tell. We are searching. And no one, including any of our family across the country, is answering any of us."

Benny made himself take a deep breath and push back the panic from that thought. He figured this might have been citywide, not worldwide.

That thought threatened to crack his cold, hard shell and he pushed it back down.

What the hell had happened?

He took another deep breath, then asked the same question again out loud.

"What the hell happened?"

"Are they all dead?" the young college-age girl asked, the look of panic in her blue eyes.

Benny had seen that look a number of times in soldiers' eyes in Iraq. She was about to flip and he wanted no part of that.

"They might be," Benny said. "I'd head off the island, get away from the city."

The professor-guy nodded.

"We can't drive and the subways aren't working," the girl said, her voice higher than a moment ago.

She was very close to going into complete panic.

The guy who seemed in charge of his little group said softly, "Let's walk."

He turned them toward the river. They stumbled in the direction he got them started in.

Then he looked back at Benny. "You coming?"

"Got to check on a few people first," Benny said.

He had no one to check on, but it was an easy lie to get out of going with them.

"We'll head south if you want to join us," the long-haired guy said.

"Thanks," Benny said to him. "I might."

Benny reached into his wallet and handed the guy his card. "Cell phone number. Call me if you hear anything or end up back this way if the phones are still working."

Benny had no intention at that moment of joining anyone, but better to leave the options open. At least this group seemed to be holding together, except for the girl.

The older guy nodded and tucked Benny's card into a pocket. "Good luck," the older guy said and followed his little flock.

Benny was starting to think it was the human race that needed the luck now. No one online, no emergency declared, and no announcements coming across any emergency bands or over the radio.

From anywhere on the planet.

Benny had a hunch that no help was coming. That group could walk all the way to Florida and never find help, other than other survivors.

Benny stood and looked around at all the death surrounding him. He had a hunch the human race had just bought the farm in a really big way.

Clearly being down in the subway had saved a number of people, and him being in his vault had saved him from whatever killed all these people.

It hadn't been gas and it hadn't been an attack. That much was clear. He had read an article last month about some huge burst of energy that might take out the entire planet coming from some other sun. Maybe something like that had happened without warning.

Or maybe this had been an alien attack.

That thought made him smile. He had clearly watched far too many late-night movies. Maggie really liked those old bug-eyed monster movies. He had really liked when she sat on his couch watching television, giving him occasional glimpses of those wonderful white panties. It had been a fair trade.

He was fairly certain he was never going to know the answer to the question of what happened. And to be honest, he didn't much care. What he did care about was staying alive now that he had drawn the lucky straw.

He headed toward Broadway along 42nd Street, working his way among the bodies.

A number of dogs, still attached to their leashes were dead as well, but he caught a glimpse of a few cats still moving. So whatever had killed the humans had spared the cats. Strange.

Near some garbage cans he also saw a number of dead rats. Thankfully he wasn't going to have to deal with those.

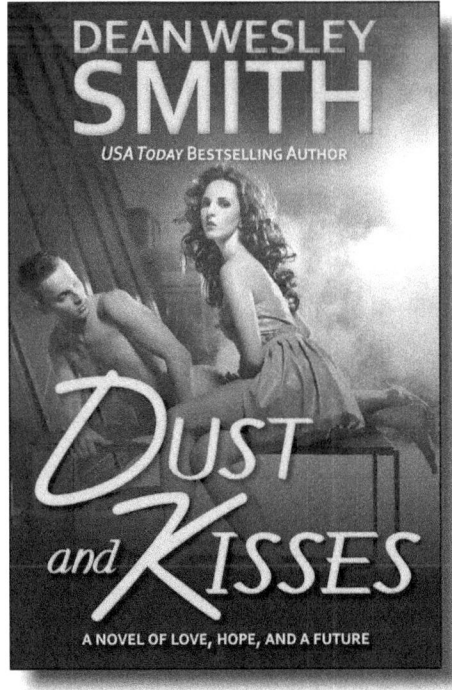

He kept walking, just looking at everything, trying to get himself calmed down, if that was even slightly possible.

What was really creepy about the bodies was the lack of blood. All the bodies he had seen in the past had become bodies because of holes that let out a lot of blood. No one sprawled on the sidewalk had any more than a bump on the head or a slight bloody face from hitting their nose when they fell.

He wandered all the way over to Broadway, seeing only a few survivors picking their way through the streets of dead. He didn't talk with any of them, but instead turned and went up Broadway.

He had no idea why. He just needed to explore, see the city he loved totally dead, help the reality sink in completely.

Finally, a couple hours later, as the sun was starting to set, he found himself back at his loan company on Lexington.

It had been a nice little business, funded by investors to help those on the streets that needed help to get by with short-term, interest-free loans. He had felt good running the little shop, helping out people, and Madge had been fantastic at getting the business grants and donors to keep everything going.

He went into his little business and pulled both Madge and Maggie out onto the sidewalk and sat them with their backs against the front of the business, like they were looking out over the street on a cool summer's evening. He smoothed down Maggie's dress so her white panties didn't show.

He had been around enough dead bodies to know that in short order they would start smelling. No point in having Marge and Maggie smell up his office.

He stood on the sidewalk and looked in both directions, suddenly realizing something that was very obvious. This entire city was going to be one stinking mess quicker than he wanted to think about. It was scheduled to not get hot for a week, which would help a little.

But not that much.

He had smelled his share of three-or-four-day-dead human bodies and didn't much care for it.

Yet in a city full of the dead, where could he go?

Where could he go in a world full of dead?

Chapter Four

AFTER TALKING WITH the others for an hour or so, Gina had gone back to her apartment on the ship and the office in her apartment.

The apartment seemed, for the first time in a while, empty. She wished she had someone to talk with, to share all this with, but she didn't. In two hundred years, she had only had a dozen relationships, all fairly long-term, but none of them had really been right for her.

And none of them had been with other Seeders, so after a few years, since she didn't age, she had always moved on.

So now she lived alone and seldom dated. Being embedded in less-advanced cultures for a decade or two per mission sort of kept the possibility of relationships down. And she had gotten used to that fact.

Most of the time, she actually liked it that way.

Helping others was worth it to her. That was her passion and what had made her sign up for this job. She sure didn't need the money anymore, since she hadn't spent hardly anything besides apartment costs in the last few hundred years.

But she didn't do this for the money. She did this as a calling, to help people improve themselves.

But on days like today, having someone close would have been nice.

She had the lights come up to just under bright and brought up some lively dance music as background to lighten her mood.

Her apartment was comfortable, with a small living room furnished in what she liked to call graduate school comfort. Huge overstuffed chairs, a long, deep couch, and a coffee table stacked high with reading material and files. One wall of the living room was a large screen, the other walls were covered in various cultures' art she had liked from her different missions.

She mostly used the living room for reading or watching movies she had collected from different planets. The apartment also had a nice kitchen where she cooked basic meals and a small bedroom. Another room off to one side of the living room functioned as her office.

The walls of her office were also decorated with pictures and art from various planets.

And some images of people, of children, families, she had helped along the way.

The apartment felt a lot like the one she had lived in while going to college on her home world to get her degrees in social science. But that apartment had been in a six-story building just down the hill from the university while this apartment was on a massive starship.

She had been on board the *Star Conscious* now for six months and the ship would remain in orbit being a support for all the embedded Seeders going into the planet below. She was glad of that, since that way she could come and go from this apartment when she wanted over the next ten years.

That would help her stay level, she knew, during the coming mission.

She now sat in her office, using a grid system over the island covered by the massive city below. That was her area, that island, and all the survivors on it.

That room she had been in as the ship first arrived in orbit would hold most of the survivors from that island city that the locals called Manhattan. But before the rest of the ships got here, she needed to track and make sure she knew where every person on the island was, so no one got missed.

She would put a tracker on each person in the *Star Conscious* computer for the extraction moment. The tracker was nothing more than a recording of each person's biometric signature and general location. The computer would do the rest in tracking them.

Right now, as the evening started to settle over the dead city on the surface and the automatic lights came on, most of the survivors had settled down. Only a few were still moving around, so it was easier for her to start tagging the survivors.

Her equipment in her office could allow her to zoom right in on each person, so close she could see facial expressions and often read their lips as to what they were saying.

She didn't think she would need to get in that close on any of the survivors. At least not this soon after the disaster. She just needed to start putting tracking on them, putting their biometric signatures into the computer so that they would not be missed.

She knew she was in for a long night.

The idea that she might miss someone just scared her to death.

An idea of what dreams she might have if she tried to sleep scared her even more.

Chapter Five

BENNY WENT BACK inside his office as night started to take over and sat in his chair behind his desk. He put up his feet and tried to think while keeping the cold of the "emotion screen," as his counselor called it, in place. Breaking down now might just end up getting him as dead as everyone else.

Outside the car alarms had calmed down some and the city was actually much quieter than he ever remembered hearing it, even late at night.

He looked around at the business he had put his heart into since getting out of the service and sighed. "Not much to do here. I think you need to figure out what to do with the next part of your life, Benny. Right?"

No one answered. His voice just echoed and that seemed damn creepy as well.

He stood and headed back out into the light of the city. Luckily, the electrical systems were still working, the stoplights still going through their cycles over piles of wrecked cars. The streetlights and building lights still made the night in the city seem like daylight. That was one of the many things he loved about this city. It never really got dark.

Now, more than likely, that wouldn't last very long without people maintaining the power systems and lines. First good

heat wave of the summer and this place would be a smelling pile of dead meat without electricity.

He headed the five blocks to his apartment, walking carefully around the bodies.

His apartment, a place he liked in most times, felt unusually silent. He clicked on the television, hoping to find something or someone to tell him what happened.

Nothing.

Some stations that had automatic programming were running, but the rest were just dead air.

The radio was the same, so he finally tuned the radio to an automatic light jazz station and let it play just to have some background music to pretend that society still existed outside the walls.

Then, using his computer, another appliance that would soon be worthless, he pulled up some maps of the New York area and the area going south.

After an hour of studying those maps, he decided the idea was too stupid for words. Assuming he made the hike all the way to Florida, even taking some cars once he was outside of the city, what was he going to do down there with the alligators and snakes and rotting-in-the-sun bodies?

"Think, Benny, think!"

He couldn't think of one darned thing. Nothing.

Then he figured he could go north, get away from all people in the woods, but he had never been one for camping. If he was going to rough it without power, he was going to do it in a plush apartment or suite. Bears shit in the woods, he liked indoor plumbing if he had a choice.

He then decided to make sure going south was as bad an idea as he had a hunch it was.

He started dialing friends he knew in Southern California from the service, another friend in Chicago from his college days, even an old girlfriend in Texas.

Again nothing.

He even dialed five of his old buddies who were still stationed overseas.

Not a one answered.

He dialed twenty people in total.

All machines or no answer.

Not rock-solid proof things were bad everywhere, but adding in the internet and television silence, enough for him.

He pushed the phone away and made himself take a deep breath, to make sure the panic would stay down.

Then he grabbed a yellow pad and asked, "What are you going to need to survive this summer and the following winter?"

Then he started making a list.

—He was going to need power for lights and air-conditioning and heat for long term.

—He was going to somehow need to figure out a way to get a place that he could hold back most of the smell until that passed, which was going to take some time and help from mother nature.

The bodies on the street would eventually dry out and mummify, which wouldn't smell as bad, but then when the rains came, the smell would return for a time.

—He was going to need a place to store food and lots of canned supplies.

—And considering the nut cases in this town that might still be alive, he was going to need a place he could protect.

—And from the faint glow out his window from the building on fire ten blocks up the street, he would need a place that wouldn't easily burn.

Maybe he could get a band of other survivors together who could work together to search for food and for defense.

He liked the sound of that.

He walked over to the window and stared toward the center of the city.

He stood there for a moment until suddenly he saw it.

The answer was right there in front of him. He knew exactly the place that fit the bill perfectly.

The Empire State Building.

Perfect.

He cooked himself a good steak dinner from his fridge and scanned the television and radio channels again as he ate, coming up blank yet again. Nothing was working besides automatic systems and those weren't going to last long at all.

Then he put on a light jacket with his trusty .45 in one pocket along with a flashlight and headed out.

At night, even with the lights of the city still completely on, the bodies looked even stranger piled and sprawled on the sidewalk.

He figured the Empire State Building had pretty much everything he would need. It was a secured building so he could defend it, it would have a pretty fine security system and extra supply of weapons for the guards, and it would have generators. In fact, he was betting it had lots of generators to run all those elevators in power failures.

He seemed to remember that the building had a lot of different elevators. Also it was high enough and windy enough that even at the worst of the smell, it should be survivable up high in the building with windows sealed.

The biggest problem was going to be clearing out the bodies that had died inside. He was going to need to do that quickly as soon as he made sure the building actually did have everything he needed.

It took him a good hour winding his way through the dead to reach the Empire State Building.

He stopped a block away and looked up at it. The damn building was a lot bigger than he remembered it.

Securing it was a crazy idea, but considering the situation, a crazy idea was exactly what he needed.

Chapter Six

GINA WORKED at her desk and monitor for almost five hours straight with only occasional breaks to get more coffee. She had three screens, one of which showed a map of the big island and the streets of the city, another had a simpler map with red dots showing each survivor.

And her main screen had an image full of green dots, showing which survivors she had tagged.

In those hours, she had managed to get the biometric signatures of every survivor she could find in the dead city, watching the number of red dots shrink as the green dots increased.

As the next day went by, the heat signatures of survivors would help her find even more, she knew.

She glanced at her screen and the green dots scattered around the island, almost all not moving. There were three hundred and sixty survivors still on the island.

For the next ten days she would have to monitor the entire area carefully to make sure to include anyone who came and went.

All over the ship she knew that others were also having long nights, working to track every survivor in their areas.

Four other large starships were now in orbit with the *Star Conscious*, three of them Seeder ships. All five ships were working on the same task she was doing over various parts of the world. There were billions dead, but by best estimates, over two million survivors.

Their mission was to not miss a person for this rescue from the second deadly electromagnetic pulse. If they rescued everyone, it would give the population of this planet a huge jump forward in a restart.

She spent another fifteen minutes going over everything, making sure she hadn't missed anyone for the night.

She hadn't.

Now she had to get some rest somehow. She would come back to this in a few hours as the sun came up over the city below and start tracking closely all of the people below to see their situations.

She dumped out the last of her cold coffee, slipped into her exercise clothes, and jumped to the ship's gym. It was a huge room with a hundred different machines, a very long running track, a climbing wall, and courts for various racket games. She liked the weight machines and did a quick fifteen-minute workout alone. She almost never had the big exercise area to herself. It felt good.

And eerily silent.

When she finished, she felt better, her muscles from so much time at the machine now loose. She jumped back to her apartment and took a quick shower to try to wash away some of the day, then got into her running shorts, a light exercise shirt, and her slippers.

That was her normal evening-at-home clothes and even though this was far from a normal evening, she wanted to pretend it was.

She went with a snack plate of crackers and cheese to the big comfortable couch in her living room.

There she clicked on a comedy movie done on the last planet she had been embedded in. She had seen it before and knew it was good. Right now she needed something to clear the images of that dead city and all those bodies from her mind.

If that was ever going to be possible.

She stretched out on her couch, a soft cloth pillow under her head, a thin blanket over her legs and feet. She started up the movie and took a few crackers, munching slowly, focusing on the movie she had already seen.

Somewhere in the first third of the movie she dozed off. Thankfully, the movie playing kept most of the nightmares back.

Not all of them, but most.

Chapter Seven

BY ELEVEN in the evening, Benny had borrowed the keys off a guard's body and found the security room. It had twenty monitors that all seemed to be working.

Twenty different views of the area around the building and the lobbies. And a couple of the monitors cycled through eight images as he watched.

Nothing was moving on any of the monitors.

Nothing.

For a short time he just kept staring at them, looking from one to another, expecting something to move.

Finally he shook his head.

"Benny, you've got yourself into a real mess this time."

His voice echoed in the bedroom-sized security room.

Staring at all the bodies showing on those cameras, he almost decided to just pack and head for Florida. Or maybe he could go north into the Canadian wilderness, join the bears shitting in the woods.

Then he shook that thought away.

This city was his home and he would be damned if he was going to let the fact that most everyone was dead scare him off.

It took him another half hour in the security room to clear out the three guard's bodies filling the chairs and a fourth guard in a back break room. Then he spent an hour finding all the generators for all the floors and the ones that ran the elevators. The generators had more than enough fuel, and when that ran out, he could re-supply easily from all the cars and trucks on the street.

From a diagram in the guardroom, he could tell there was a good-sized water tank up high that had electrical pumps. He was going to have to check every room to make sure all the water was turned off so that didn't drain out when the power shut off.

The Empire State Building was all offices and meeting rooms and tourist stuff. No apartments, so he would have to find a really high office and clean that out and set up an apartment. That would be easy to do.

He hoped.

He had a hunch none of what he was thinking of doing was going to be easy.

For the next hour, he went around taking all the keys and guns from the dead guards and then locking the five main entrances to the building. That felt weird, like he was locking out the dead, but if he wanted to be secure, no point in taking any chances that some other survivors had this idea.

The last thing he needed were survivors with more guns than he had. And in New York, nut cases with guns scared him more than almost anything else.

Outside the doors, the lights of the city looked very strange on all the people scattered dead on the sidewalks.

He went back to the main security area and spent the rest of the night making sure he knew all the details of the building, or at least as much as he could find.

He didn't want to be on an elevator with no chance of rescue when the power went out. He needed to know that the back-up generators would kick in and if that didn't happen, how to do an emergency escape from the elevator. He had a hunch he was going to be spending a lot of time in those elevators. Being trapped alive in one with no chance of rescue scared him cold.

Somewhere along the way, he fell asleep for a few hours on a cot in a side room off the security area.

He didn't even remember lying down.

Chapter Eight

GINA AWOKE SWEATING on the couch, the light blanket twisted around her feet. Her mouth was dry and her short hair was plastered to her head.

She pushed away any thought of trying to remember any dream and managed to get untangled and get to her feet. The screen was blank, so the movie had ended and the system had shut down.

She clicked it off and glanced at a clock near the screen. She had been asleep for three hours. The sun would be coming up on the city below. She needed to get back to work.

She headed for the bathroom for another shower, then to her kitchen to get a few bagels with cream cheese and a large glass of orange juice. That was her breakfast of choice most mornings and it got her going.

Usually she headed to the ship's gym after breakfast to do her regular hour-long exercise routine, but today she would skip that.

Too much to do, too many lives at stake.

She got back into her office to her screens and discovered that while she had slept, five of her tagged survivors had left the island. She transferred them to the person monitoring the area they were in.

There were also six new red dots on her screen and she quickly tagged them. She had no idea where they had come from. More than likely deep underground, although her system could penetrate through a hundred feet of rock and any building.

But there was a good chance they had been farther underground than that last night.

She sat eating her breakfast while methodically checking her survivors to make sure they were tagged correctly.

She had just finished her breakfast and downed the last of her orange juice when one of her green lights winked out.

She instantly focused her tracking on it, afraid of what she might find, but knowing she had to look anyway.

The survivor had been a man about fifty. He had taken a gun to his head while sitting next to his wife and two teenage kids who had died while eating.

She felt sick, looking at the scene of death like a snooping angel.

She made a note with shaking hands that he was dead and then pulled back so she didn't have to look at the scene any more.

She knew, and everyone who was doing her job had been briefed, that over the next ten days, while they were tracking the survivors for the rescue and waiting for all the ships to arrive, many survivors would either be killed or take their own lives.

She just hadn't expected it to happen so soon.

She pushed back from her desk and took her orange juice glass and plate she had used for the bagels to the kitchen.

Then she just stood there, her head down over the sink, shaking.

She had been alive for almost two hundred years, had seen many things in the cultures she had worked, but she had no doubt the next nine days until rescue were going to be some of the longest and hardest days she had ever lived.

And then after that, it would only get worse.

After that, she would be down there, on those streets, with the survivors, trying to help.

Chapter Nine

AN ALARM WOKE Benny.

He scrambled to the screens in the main security room, at first not remembering where he was or what had happened.

Then he saw all the bodies and nothing moving. The sun was slowly bringing light to the city.

The first full day of death was dawning.

An alarm was flashing and ringing like an insane doorbell that it was time to open the doors.

He shut it off, dropping the room back into welcome silence.

He went back to the cot where he had passed out a few hours before and clicked on a radio there. It gave him no more hope than it had yesterday.

Outside, it looked overcast and cool. That was good for the moment, since it would slow down the body decay slightly on the people in the streets.

And keep most of them from heating up in the sun, swelling, and exploding from the expanding gas inside of them. He had seen that a few times in Iraq as well.

He hoped to never see it again.

He banged open a candy machine in the break room and breakfast consisted of a couple packs of nuts and a Diet Coke.

From what he could tell from the monitors, there had to have been at least three or four hundred people in this building when humanities number came up. No way he was going to move all of them ahead of when they would start smelling.

He was just going to have to go up high, to the 102 Floor Observatory, and work his way down, clearing every body he could find from as many top floors as he could.

About a third of the way up, a person had to change elevators and there were a lot of bodies in that lobby area, so he just figured more there wouldn't hurt.

But when he got to that lobby, he decided that was a bad idea. He was going to have to go through that transition floor all the time. He needed to clear that first.

He went down three floors from the transition area and into a huge office suite. There were a good twenty bodies in the big room that he could see.

Using a large fire ax, he broke out some of the windows in an office there, letting in the morning-chilled wind from outside. The office had a door on it that he could close after he was finished.

Then, one-by-one, he dragged all the bodies in that large office area to the window and just dumped them out, leveraging them up over the edge and turning away as they fell.

After about thirty bodies, a couple of which could have used less pasta when alive, he decided he was going to need a better system. He wouldn't have a back after a short time.

Plus touching the dead bodies that much gave him the creeps.

He went down to the building mail and shipping room and got a large cart used to haul heavy boxes. Then on the service elevator, he went all the way to the top.

It took him two hours to clear the two-dozen people on the top observation deck and take them down a dozen floors to another empty office suite, where he again broke out a window in an office that could be shut tight after he was done. This time he just stacked the poor souls near the window to take care of later.

He felt bad that he wasn't treating the dead in a more respectful fashion, but at this point, his own survival was far, far more important. And that depended on getting the dead out of the building as soon as he could.

By eleven in the morning, he knew that stacking those bodies there wouldn't help his situation at all. He had to toss them outside. Which meant that by the time he got done clearing out the bodies in this building, there would be a stack of human flesh a story tall around the north base.

He would be living on a pile of the dead.

But again he could think of no other choice.

But he could toss them out only on the north side, leaving the other three sides open.

Like they used to say in the service, he was already walking dead. Not a way to keep from making a mistake and getting himself injured or killed. He was going to need more food and more rest, if that was possible before he went on.

He went back down to the security area and did a check of the area outside the building.

Just death.

No movement.

He ate a quick lunch of some guard's sandwich stored in the fridge and then took another nap. Two hours later, he was just about ready to go again when his cell phone in his pocket rang and scared hell out of him.

"Yeah," he said after he scrambled to get it to his ear.

"This is the man you met yesterday with the three college kids," the voice on the other end said.

"Find anything?" Benny asked, for a moment excited at the idea that he might have been wrong about everyone being dead.

"Nothing," the man said. "We're coming back to the city. It's where we all live, doesn't seem right leaving it. You got any ideas on where to hole up to get through the summer and all the smell?"

Benny's stomach twisted in disappointment, then he pushed that aside as he had been pushing all feeling aside since this started.

He glanced at the security cameras showing room after room of bodies and shrugged. Why not? He could use the help.

"I'm setting up the Empire State Building," Benny said. "It won't burn, it's got generators, a great security system, and a good water supply. It can be defended."

"And it's high enough to escape some of the smell," the guy said.

Benny was impressed. He had been worrying about the same thing.

"You and your merry band want to join me?" Benny asked. "There's a lot of work to do."

"It will take us about three hours to get there," the professor said. "Thanks."

"Pick up anyone else you see that looks sane along the way," Benny said. "This is one big building. And go to the South Entrance. I'll be waiting there in three hours."

"Okay," the professor said.

"And one more thing. Stay away from the building on the north side."

"Why?" he asked, then before Benny could tell him, the professor said, "Oh, I understand."

This guy really was smart. That was good. It was going to take Benny's street smarts and military training and the professor's brains to get any of them alive through the coming year.

"Three hours, call me if you get stuck or run into problems."

"Three hours," he said and hung up.

Benny once again checked the television and radio. Nothing.

At least he was going to have help.

Chapter Ten

AS THE DAY wore on, Gina was handed four survivors coming back onto the island from the south, and in turn she had handed off more than a dozen leaving the city, most headed north.

From her original three hundred and sixty, she was down to three hundred and twenty-two.

From the maps of the area, going north made sense, since in that direction was more wilderness and fewer people. It would be a lot easier in the wilderness to survive the smell of all the death that was coming.

One-by-one, she checked in on the survivors in her area. Most of them had gone home. Many were just sitting in shock next to a dead loved one.

A few were working to fortify and remove dead bodies from upper areas of apartment buildings and one man was working to remove bodies from one of the tallest buildings in the city.

There were only a few people working with another person. Almost everyone worked alone and she couldn't imagine that. It showed the really true survival ability of the human race.

The man in the big building seemed to have been moving almost constantly since she awoke and her interest kept going to him. She didn't focus in close because he was always moving dead bodies and tossing them out windows. She didn't need to see that up close, but she admired what he was doing in trying to survive.

And his strength.

She forced herself to take both a lunch break away from her screens and a dinner break. She needed to just sit in her kitchen and focus on eating and not thinking about what was happening on the planet below.

Both meals had been nothing special, just a sandwich and a drink and a piece of fruit, but it was enough.

After her dinner break, she headed to the gym again for a short workout, then, after a quick shower, she took a cup of tea back with her to the office and to watch as many survivors worked to get ready for another night.

And many, many more survivors just sat, doing nothing.

She honestly wasn't sure what she would be doing if this had happened to her home world and she had survived.

She hoped she would be one working to survive.

But she wasn't sure.

Chapter Eleven

BENNY TOOK SOME lumber from the maintenance area and went back up to the floor where he had broken out the window in the office. There he spent an hour building a ramp for the shipping cart that slanted slowly up to the broken window.

Then he went back to the floor under the top observation platform and worked his way down, room-by-room, office-by-office, floor-by-floor, using the cart to take the bodies he found to the ramp and dumping them out the window. Luckily for him, some of those floors were empty, thanks to the high rents for the place.

Or a slow day at the office.

In one office, it made him sad when he found twenty very attractive women,

slumped to the floor or over their desks. He would have dated any of them. And that thought made him miss Maggie and her white panties.

He even missed Madge.

He just hoped that some women survived besides that panicked college girl. With luck, he and other survivors would build a nice little community right here in the Empire State building.

With luck.

He found a nice hide-a-bed couch in one executive's office on the eighty-ninth floor and decided that was where he would bunk for the night later. It had a really nice bathroom and shower and he was really needing a shower after all those bodies and work.

He had had no idea how much work it was going to be to move around dead human weight. People who had done that for a living before were amazing.

Exhausted, he went downstairs to the south entrance at three hours, making sure to take the .45 tucked in his pocket.

No sign of the professor and his class, so he went across the street to a deli and got some great roast beef from the fridge and made himself a sandwich. He was really going to miss fresh meat.

He got enough food for three solid meals tomorrow and went back across the street and put the food in the fridge in the security room.

The deli had three bodies in it and another near the door, but he just didn't have the energy to do anything with the bodies at the moment. But he would have to, since that deli had a full back room of supplies and some nice freezers full of meat. He figured he could get a couple of those freezers across the street and hooked up to a generator and maybe have meat for the winter.

He was back inside the lobby of the Empire State Building and was about to lock the door when he saw the professor and his three charges winding their way along the sidewalk.

They all looked tired and clearly depressed, and the girl had lost her backpack along the way.

He propped the door open and waited for them, chewing on the roast beef sandwich with horseradish, which he had to admit, tasted wonderful.

"Thanks, Benny," the professor said, extending his hand. "My name is Professor C.M. Green." He laughed, sadly. "Not sure what I'm a professor of anymore."

He had managed to pull back his long hair and tie it, and Benny could tell the professor had been a gym rat. He was strong, of that Benny had no doubt. The professor had a firm grip, but Benny could tell that the last day had really worn on him.

Benny was fairly certain he looked just as bad.

The professor quickly introduced the two college boys. The redhead with bright freckles who stood about six foot was called David. The other kid, shorter with a lot of pimples was Freddy. Both looked like they could use some muscle and about fifty pounds. The girl was named Candice. She had long blonde hair, long fingernails, and the remains of some makeup on her blue eyes. She looked like she was about to pass out.

"You had any real food?" Benny asked them.

The professor shook his head. "Just snacks is all."

"So that's job one," Benny said.

He had them leave their stuff just inside the building entrance, tossed the professor a group of keys from a guard, locked up the building, then headed across the street to the deli.

"Boys," Benny said, "can you clear out those bodies, move them a little ways down the sidewalk, maybe about thirty steps, while the professor and I fix you something to eat."

Both boys looked horrified that they would have to touch a dead body and the professor didn't look too pleased himself.

"Do it this way," Benny said, grabbing the man's body near the door by both feet right at the ankle. Then Benny just dragged the body away from the door and down the sidewalk. The body's clothes bunched up some as Benny went, but not enough to slow him down.

"Don't try to pick them up," Benny said, still tugging on the body down the walk, "and if you don't want to use your bare hands, there's a store two doors down that has leather gloves. Bring me and the professor back two pair of larges each as well."

Benny stopped dragging the body, then led the professor and the girl into the deli as the two boys went for gloves.

"There's a lot of work to get that building ready," Benny said as they went in behind the counter.

"I can't even imagine," he said.

"You won't have to imagine," Benny said. "You're going to get to see it for yourself as soon as we're done eating."

The boys cleared out the bodies, each grabbing one leg and moving quickly. Then they all sat and ate sandwiches with cold pop.

The professor described how far they had walked before turning back. They had stayed the night in a furniture store, but most of them hadn't slept much.

All of them had families they were convinced were dead, and the professor had a wife. "We're all going to need to find our families and check on them," he said. "It's why we came back."

Benny nodded. His only family had been Madge and Maggie. Both his parents had died in a boating accident while he was in Iraq. He knew Maggie and Madge were dead. He would have looked for them as well if he hadn't known. Especially Maggie.

"I can understand that," Benny said.

The professor nodded thanks.

"Any idea at all what caused this?" Benny asked as the conversation lagged.

"Quasar pulse," Freddy said.

"Aliens," David said.

The professor shook his head. "All kinds of theories, no facts."

Benny nodded. "Well back to the task of survival then. We need to get as much of the building cleared and set up before things turn really sour."

"You mean everything smells?" Candice asked.

"Worse than you can imagine," Benny said. "We'll work some more tonight, and then we all need some rest."

He turned to the professor. "How about tomorrow you take a student and go out one at a time to find that person's family? And maybe look for more sane people to join us. The rest of us will keep working."

"That's a really good plan," the professor said, trying and failing to sound upbeat. "Everyone up for that?"

They all just nodded and kept eating.

If nothing else, this was the most well-behaved and smallest class Benny had ever seen.

Chapter Twelve

GINA WATCHED after dinner as the four that had come back into the city joined the man working alone in the big building. Somehow they had known he was there. Maybe related or something and able to get in touch.

So far, all the systems in the city seemed to be staying up. But as the night fell over the city for the second time since all the death, Gina knew that it wouldn't be long before those lights would never come on again.

But pulling back, the view from above of the island city was stunning at night, the city looking alive and vibrant, at least from orbit.

As the sun started to fall, she had green lights wink and go dark on her board.

She checked each one because she had to. It was her job.

Six total. Three had gone to a roof of a building and just walked off the edge.

She knew this was happening all over the planet right now. She just wished they could get the survivors off faster, give them some hope, if not just for a moment.

But right now there were less than twenty ships in orbit over all the death. She knew there would need to be almost a thousand ships to get all the survivors, and many of those rescue ships wouldn't arrive until the last minute. Many were coming from another sector of this galaxy at full speed.

After another two hours, all the survivors in her area seemed to have settled down, including the five now together in the big building. So she went and took another shower to try to clear away the day, then went to her couch again and started up the same comedy movie she had on the night before.

She didn't need to be entertained. She just needed noise and some life.

She fell asleep in twenty minutes.

And the only dream she had that she could remember was of watching a person's face with a green light on the person's forehead. Then the light winked out and the person slumped to the ground.

And she had to turn away and do nothing, because there was nothing she could do.

Chapter Thirteen

AFTER FINISHING the sandwiches and closing up the deli, Benny took the professor and his charges up to the security room and made sure they all knew the same things he did about the emergency generators and how to escape if stuck in an elevator when the power went out.

Then pulling the professor aside, Benny suggested that the two boys start working on clearing out the main lobbies downstairs, dragging the bodies away from the main doors and down the sidewalk a distance, that sort of thing. And that the professor and Candice start on the floor Benny had left off hauling bodies out, check every bathroom and lunchroom in every office to make sure the water was turned off. Even the public bathrooms in the lobbies and if there were any sinks or bathrooms in any basement areas.

"What are you going to do?" the professor asked after he sent the two boys off with their assignments and instructions to call him on his cell if they needed him.

"I am going to keep working my way down clearing bodies."

The professor just nodded.

Benny decided that first the three of them needed to go all the way back to the top, then start down from there, double-checking to make sure he hadn't missed any body in a maintenance area, or in a back office or rest room, and that all the water was turned off on those upper floors.

Benny showed the professor and Candice his cart set-up and ramp in the office with the broken window when they reached that floor.

Neither said a word.

Then the two of them went off checking the water and Benny kept working his way down, one body, one floor at a time. By the time two hours had gone by and the lights of the city were on full, Benny had the top thirty floors completely cleared of bodies.

And he was exhausted. He knew they all were.

He had scouted the neighborhood a little, mostly with the exterior security cameras, and he knew there was another restaurant nearby, so all five of them headed there to scrounge for food.

A couple stores down from the restaurant, they found bedding, and in a neighboring store they all found a change of clothes.

They cleared the bodies out of both places in only minutes, since Benny figured they were going to need to use both places in the future.

Benny was starting to feel better by the minute.

It had only been a little over a day since the world ended and he had a hunch this new way of living just might work. They all might actually have a way to survive, with enough help.

And a little more time with the weather staying cool and the power staying on.

Benny doubted that would happen, but he figured a guy could hope.

Chapter Fourteen

OVER THE NEXT few days, Gina fell into a routine. She would crawl off the couch and check on the survivors in her city, finding any that had died in the night, and seeing if she had anyone new, or if others had left the city.

After the third day, all the others who were doing her job for other areas under the *Star Conscious* had a meeting. There were forty of them and they all looked as tired and worn out as she was feeling.

The upshot of the meeting was that after three days, every survivor on the planet had been identified by all the ships in orbit and tagged. As soon as the other ships got here, the survivors would be taken off the planet and out of danger for the time of the second electromagnetic pulse.

They were told to start getting to know the survivors who looked like they would make it, the ones they could help, to figure out the best way to help the survivors after the rescue.

She wasn't willing to do that just yet. Too many were still dying.

By the fourth day, she had under three hundred survivors alive on the island. And she knew that a few more of them didn't have much longer to live, since they hadn't been eating or moving in days.

The five survivors in the big building she still watched from a distance, and four others in another tall building were

working on it to clear bodies and make it livable. More than likely that would be the two groups she would work to help.

All the other survivors huddled inside apartments or underground in the subway system, some setting up camps in the stalled trains.

Except for checking on those that died, she kept her focus above the city, thinking of each person at the moment as a green light. That helped her nightmares some.

And she didn't have to see the bodies that littered everything slowly starting to decompose.

She was going to embed in that city to help the survivors, and right now, she refused to think about what that smell was going to be like.

Since all Seeders could teleport, she would be able to return to her apartment here at any point, but she had no doubt that would not be enough by any stretch.

She knew those survivors below would need her help after the rescue. She knew that deep down. But she had no idea why she had applied to do this.

Chapter Fifteen

BENNY WAS STUNNED that Mother Nature and the electric company conspired to help them some. It remained fairly cool, the nights almost chilly, and the power stayed on.

For five days, he and the Professor and his charges prepared the big building as much as they could.

After a few hundred bodies dumped through windows, Benny was just numb to what he was doing.

And after the first few days, they

were all wearing masks and tossing their clothes out after working. Every night Benny took a long, hot shower to try to clear the smell from his nose.

They finally got every body they could find out of the big building by day four. Benny was stunned it had been done. It was a very large building.

The city was starting to smell in general, so after clearing the bodies from the entire building, Benny turned their focus to stocking up on bedding, food, clothing, and just about anything else they thought they might need and could get on carts or carry.

Pretty soon they would just lock the doors and move up into the top floors. And after the power went out, they would run the generators for those floors, keeping them at a comfortable temperature through the summer.

Benny took the top office floor as his apartment, and the professor and his three kids stocked up the floor five down from his, since there were six bathrooms and lots of offices that could be made into bedrooms there.

From what Benny understood, they had spread out and each had a large area and a private bathroom.

Benny wanted them to be prepared for fifty or more people living in the building instead of just five, even though they hadn't seen anyone else in days. And the professor agreed.

So even after they had more than enough, they stocked food and blankets and propane heaters and lighting and everything else on a dozen different floors.

One day, David asked Benny why they were doing that.

"The moment the lights go out," Benny said, "and we keep some lights on in this building up high, people from all over will see us. We need to be ready for people to join us."

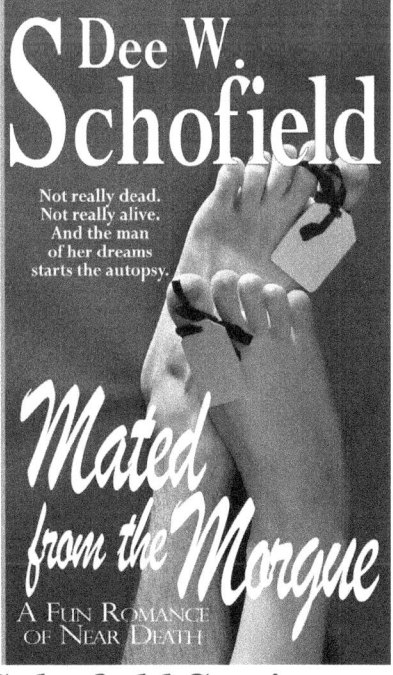

David had only nodded to that.

All the kids and the professor had found their families, all dead.

And every-so-often Benny would run across one of the kids crying. Nothing he could say to cheer them up. They were either going to make it or they weren't.

He had become very cold through all this, much more than he had ever been before.

His counselor had taught him that. He had decided after that session with the counselor that Benny would be one of the soldiers that made it.

And he would make it this time as well.

The young girl, Candice, just slowly withdrew, working and eating less and less, no matter what any of them said or tried to do to cheer her up.

Benny had seen that before in soldiers on the battlefield. He had no idea what to do about it.

On the fifth morning she vanished, going out the south door before any of them got up.

Benny had no doubt she wouldn't be back, but the professor wanted to go in search of her.

Benny stopped him at first with one simple statement speech. "It's safe out there. She knows where we are. If she wants to come back, she will. Give her until tomorrow before we go looking for her."

Benny doubted she would return, but he might be wrong. He hoped he would be.

The professor agreed and gave her the time and didn't go out looking for her. But the next day he and the boys went out into the smell. The professor said they had to do something.

Benny knew that feeling as well.

But it was one damn big city out there full of dead people, so he held out no hope.

Chapter Sixteen

GINA JUST HAPPENED to be at her screens, watching the survivors green dots when one of the five from the big building in the center of town left. The other four didn't seem to be moving.

She focused her scan down on the moving survivor, surprised to find she was watching a young college-age girl wearing a mask against the smell, winding her way through the dead bodies on the street.

The young girl seemed to be staggering more than walking and Gina didn't like the looks of that at all.

Gina focused in on the girl's face as much as she could and could see the look of shock and despair in the girl's eyes. This girl was going off to die, Gina had no doubt.

And there was still a good five days until the rescue.

Gina followed the girl for the next hour as she worked through the bodies, finally entering a large building with no survivors in it.

The girl went up the elevator to the eleventh floor and into an apartment there.

Gina could see there were two bodies in the apartment, both still in fairly decent shape because the air-conditioning in the apartment must have still been working.

Gina watched as the young girl sat down on the couch facing where one man sprawled on the floor and a woman lay sprawled in the kitchen.

The girl sat there for a few minutes, then went down the hall to a bedroom and crawled into a bed that must have clearly been hers before the disaster.

She pulled the blankets up to her chin and closed her eyes.

Gina knew exactly what had happened.

The young girl had gone home to be with her dead parents.

Gina switched back to the four others in the big building and for the first time focused down on them.

Two were young boys about the girl's age, another was a man with long hair, and the fourth man just flat took her breath away.

It was if an electrical shock had come through the screen and pushed her back in her chair.

He was clearly the one in charge. He had short dark hair and had shaved, something many of the survivors had not done. He wore jeans and a muscle shirt that clearly showed off how strong he was.

She glanced back at her records. He was the one that had first started cleaning out the building on his own.

She just stared at him, stunned that she was having such a reaction. Normally a man never really caught her attention. Over the last few centuries, there had been a few that had twisted her heart, and a dozen or more short relationships, but never had she felt a reaction like this to just seeing a man.

After a short discussion as Gina watched, they all nodded and seemed to go back to work.

Gina figured that they knew where the girl had gone and were going to give her time. That was the right decision for someone in shock and mourning as that young girl clearly was.

Gina followed them, becoming more impressed by the minute that all four of them were fine, now working to build a future in the big building.

As she followed them, they went out into the city streets and worked to get more bedding, more food, more supplies from nearby stores.

All four of them had carts and they worked to stock floors where they did not live.

Clearly one of them, more than likely the man she could barely keep her eyes off of, was setting up the big building to hold a lot more than five.

Wow, he was good-looking.

And clearly smart.

She spent the next hour just watching him like she was beside him.

And for the first time, she actually wanted to be down there, in all that death, talking with him, getting to know him.

How was that even possible?

Chapter Seventeen

THE POWER cut out on the tenth day and, as Benny had expected, the heat started to climb to oppressive levels, making going outside into all the death just about impossible.

All the bodies along the sidewalks were bloated inside their cloths and impossible to look at. Benny again just thanked the luck that the rats and other rodents had all been killed. Otherwise, there would have been no staying in the city with the rats having unlimited food supply.

Benny had them all go to using propane lanterns and climbing stairs. He didn't want to take any chances at this point on elevators run by a generator until they tested everything. They could do that tomorrow.

Benny had set up a portable generator on a balcony outside of the office suite that he had converted to a very large apartment, with a big screen television and a movie library that would take him ten years to watch if he never stopped.

He had all the staircases boarded and sealed on his floor except for one, and that one he had steel bars locking it at night. And he had no doubt he had enough firepower to hold off a pretty good-sized attack.

Not that he thought one was coming. He actually doubted it was, but in the Gulf he had seen his share of the underside of humanity. And New York clearly had its share as well. He had survived this, which meant scum might have as well. Not everyone was going to be nice guys like the professor and his kids.

When the power went out, Benny made sure all outside and front doors were locked again, then set up alarms in the security room that would ring on his floor and the professor's floor if anyone banged on the outside door.

He also set up the exterior and lobby camera systems with motion sensors to run on generators. If anything at all moved near a door, the alarm would sound and they would see who it was.

Four days before, while it was still fairly cool out, the professor and the boys had gone out looking for Candice. They had come back depressed and smelling so bad, Benny just let them go take showers without a word.

The next day, because the two boys were still depressed, Benny and the professor went out again, without luck.

Candice had vanished.

Benny felt bad, but it didn't surprise him. Some people were survivors, others were not.

On the day after the power went out, over a light lunch, they got talking about what had happened again and what was going to happen.

"The aliens will come to rescue us," David said.

Benny shook his head and asked David, "Why would you say that?"

David shrugged. "They've been taking our kind to another planet for centuries. They knew we would be destroyed. They planned for it and will come back to help us."

"And you know all this how?" Benny asked as the professor just smiled, clearly having heard all this before.

"He doesn't," Freddy said. "If the aliens caused all this, they just missed a few of us and will be back to finish the job so they will have the planet to themselves."

"No, they will rescue us," David said.

"Kill us," Freddy said.

The professor said nothing.

Benny quickly changed the subject.

Chapter Eighteen

FOR THE LAST four days before the rescue, Gina no longer dreamed of death, but of the man with the black hair, dark eyes, and strong arms.

He seemed almost scary smart in how he went about preparing the big building. She was so looking forward to meeting him, but she wasn't sure what she was going to say. And that made her feel like a young kid again back in school.

She hadn't felt that way in two hundred years.

Besides what could she say after he had lived through those ten days? "Hi, I'm an alien and I'm here to rescue you for only a few hours before putting you back?"

She would have to think of something much better than that.

A lot better.

And then after she went to the surface to help them, she would have to think of yet another way to meet him.

But meet him twice she would. She was going to make sure of that.

Three days after the young girl left the group in the big building, it was clear she was never going back. The long-haired man and the two younger boys went out looking for her wearing gas masks to help hold back the smell.

Gina watched them carefully every step.

The first place they had gone was to where the young girl was hiding. They clearly had known her home address.

When the young girl had heard them coming, she had hid under her bed, curled inside a blanket. She did not want to be found.

Gina yelled at her screens, trying to shout through space that all they had to do was look under the bed. The girl was there and she needed help.

The long-haired man and the two boys didn't see her and left.

For an instant Gina considering jumping to the girl's apartment and making a lot of noise so the long-haired man and the two boys would return, but all the people in her job had strict orders to not go to the surface until after the rescue.

So she just watched.

When they left, the young girl got back out from under the bed and crawled back into bed, pulling the blankets over her head.

She had been eating some, so she would survive until rescue, but not much

longer. Gina would try to do something to help her after rescue.

Gina looked at the tally of the green lights in her area. Just over two hundred and eighty survivors left.

But over half of those were alone just as the young girl was. They would make it to rescue, but not much longer after that when they were returned.

After the rescue, when Gina embedded on the surface, she might be able to find and help more of them besides the blonde girl. But she wondered if they even wanted help.

She would have to figure out which ones did want help during the rescue. And work with those. Maybe get them to the big building run by the most handsome man she had ever seen.

On the day before the rescue, she went to the big banquet-like room where all the survivors from her area would be transported. It would hold them, without problem.

She double-checked on setting up showers that had special chemicals in the water to kill the smell. She made sure that all of them would have fresh clothing if they wanted it. And she worked with the medical staff to make sure there would be enough help there for the injured and those who needed to be sedated.

The extremely injured and near dead would not be sent back to the surface, but instead would be taken as refugees to another nearby planet. But everyone else would be sent back.

One wall of the big room was clear and looked out at the beautiful planet below. That view would help some of the survivors realize where they were.

Others, she knew, that view would shock. Again, medical would be ready.

Almost all of the survivors in her area would be asleep when they were taken, since the time would be right before sunrise. That would help some as well, she hoped.

The entire rescue was going to only take about ten hours.

Ten very long hours for some survivors, ten very short hours for others. But none of them would remember it.

She went back to her apartment and got ready for the rescue, making careful notes of the locations of everyone and what they looked like so she could talk with them when they arrived.

If she was going to help these people, she had a lot of work to do both before and after they arrived in that big room.

THE RESCUE

Chapter Nineteen

ONE MOMENT BENNY had been sound asleep on the big bed he had managed to get into the top floor office complex, the next he found himself standing beside the professor and the two boys with hundreds of other very tired and scared-looking humans who had survived the destruction of the world.

Some were wearing full clothes, others were wearing very little. Clearly all of them had been as asleep as he had been.

Luckily, he had been sleeping in sweat pants and a body shirt just in case. The light carpet under his bare feet was warm and slightly soft.

The room, at first glance, seemed like a normal hotel banquet room.

He looked quickly around him, but saw no real danger, just a bunch of very confused, sick, and smelly people.

"What the hell?" Benny asked, more to himself than anyone.

"We're in orbit above our city," David said, pointing at the big wall.

Benny turned and damn near dropped to the floor as his knees got wobbly.

They were in orbit.

Holy shit!

How had he got here?

Or someone had done a pretty good fake show of being in orbit on a huge wall. He wanted to try to believe that, but he knew he couldn't.

He was in orbit.

He could see that sunrise was working its way across the Atlantic toward the East Coast and there were very few clouds in the sky, meaning it was going to be a hot summer's day below if what he was seeing was real.

A very large if.

His mind would not accept it.

Could not accept it.

"That's amazing," Freddy said, his voice almost a whisper.

"I was right," David said. "The aliens are here to rescue us."

"Perfect," Benny said, staring out that window as more people around them noticed the view as well. "Are we in the frying pan or in the fire?"

"I'm guessing fire," the professor said.

"We're lunch," Freddy said.

"I doubt they have a cookbook," David said.

Benny had no idea what they were talking about, but it didn't sound good that they suddenly found themselves in orbit in a ship and the two kids who liked science fiction were talking about aliens eating humans.

The noise and the smell stunned him as the people in the room started to shout and panic a little.

Numbers of people just fainted or dropped to the carpeted floor and sat there, their hands covering their faces.

Benny made himself take a deep breath and actually look around.

Except for the giant wall looking out into space, this room could have been any banquet room in any hotel. High ceilings with off-white paint, overhead lights, carpet on the floor.

Benny pushed back the feeling of panic trying to creep up his throat. He wasn't sure what there was to panic about, since most of the planet below had already been wiped out.

He honestly wasn't sure what could be worse, but he had a hunch he was about to find out.

Then one of the doors on one side of the room slid back and a dozen more people strode into the room.

They were far from alien.

In fact, one woman looked directly at him and then nodded and smiled as if she knew him.

He managed to catch his breath.

He was on an alien ship, after the world had ended, and he was having a reaction to some woman who walked into the room.

A real reaction.

A lust reaction.

All of the new arrivals looked as human as he was, only they were all clearly more rested and clean.

The woman wore a white blouse with the sleeves rolled up, jeans, and tennis shoes. She had really short, black hair and skin that contrasted with the black hair. She didn't seem to be any older than he was.

And she clearly worked out.

Around Benny the room quieted and calmed some as everyone turned to watch the new arrivals.

The woman with the short black hair stood to one side of the stage, clearly concerned as she looked around at everyone. One man jumped up on a low stage. You could have heard the old pin drop in that room, even on the carpeted floor.

The guy looked totally human. He had on a dress shirt, business slacks, and dress shoes. He could have been one of the Wall Street clones on a day off for all Benny could tell.

"Fine people of the great city of New York," he said in perfect English. "Very sorry to startle you like this from your sleep. What caused the disaster you have been living through was a pulsar blast of intense electromagnetic radiation. The next, and final wave off the pulsar will be hitting Earth in just under four hours. We have almost a thousand ships circling the planet pulling all who survived the first pulsar wave to safety."

"Pulsar?" someone shouted.

"Yes, a very powerful electromagnetic wave from a nearby star is what hit your planet ten days ago. All of you survived because you were protected in some fashion, either underground or behind thick steel walls."

Benny nodded, as did others around him. As he figured, the vault had saved him.

"How come you couldn't get here before the first wave?" one guy shouted.

"And who are you, anyway?" someone else shouted.

The man looked pained and Benny could see a deep sadness in his eyes. He clearly felt the loss of life as much as anyone.

"Let's just say I'm as human as the rest of you," the man said, "and from a very distant place. We were not able to save anyone or block the first pulsar wave, but we can save all of you who survived and let the second and final wave pass with no more deaths. Then you will all be put back on Earth to rebuild."

"What happens if we don't want to go back to that graveyard?" one woman shouted.

A lot of people shouted "Yeah, what happens?"

Again the man smiled and said, "We'll come to that problem when the time comes. But for now, there is food and drink against the far wall and cots to take naps. There are showers for those of you who would like one, and fresh changes of clothes. This entire process will take about ten hours. Please relax and I will be back to talk with you as soon as I can. I have other rooms of survivors I must address."

"One last question," the professor beside me shouted at the man. "How many survived the first wave?"

"Worldwide," the man said, smiling, "almost two million. And we'll get them all, I promise."

As the noise of three hundred people talking at once filled the room like a hard wave, Benny turned to David who had been talking about the aliens.

"Well, now what?"

"I have no idea," he said, his eyes wide.

At that moment, a girl's voice called out, "Professor," and Candice hit the professor's hug, sobbing.

Benny was glad to see she was still alive, but not as much as the boys in her class. She looked like she had gone through hell, and she smelled awful, like she had been sitting next to a dead body for days.

"Where have you been?" the professor asked, clearly fantastically glad to see her.

"At my apartment," she said between sobs.

That made sense. She had simply gone home to die beside her parents.

The owners of this big ship in orbit clearly were going to make sure that didn't happen.

At least not for the next ten hours.

Chapter Twenty

GINA WAS STUNNED. The man was more handsome in person than on her screens, if that was possible. And he had clearly been stunned when he saw her. But she had no idea how she was going to meet him.

But for the moment, that didn't matter. She had just under three hundred people in this big room she had to take care of. After Chairman Carson finished his introduction and left, she started to work.

First, she made sure the medical staff were dealing with as many of the injured and weak as possible. A good fifty people had just slumped to the floor when they arrived and looked to be in bad condition.

Medical had a few dozen smaller rooms set up to one side of the large room and forty of her people were moving the injured away.

Other ship members were spreading out food along one wall and still others were helping survivors to private showers.

A lot of people stood alone, just looking around, scared to death. Others had grouped up and were talking.

Gina made sure that she quickly had people talking with every solo person, moving them toward a group of other survivors if possible.

And Gina, at times, recorded her impressions of different people as she worked her way around the room. She was going to need to work with and try to help a large number of these people over the next few years. She was only one person and seeing everyone still in the city below packed into one room, it felt overwhelming to her.

And sad at the same time. The entire remaining population of a once great city now fit into one banquet room.

She pushed that thought away and went back to work. She knew that a large share of these people would not find a way to survive the summer. And that made her mad because she wanted to try to help everyone here.

But it became very clear as the medical staff moved more and more people away to smaller rooms that a lot of people just didn't want to be helped or survive.

She had never been a person who gave up on anything, but she couldn't imagine what the people in this room had gone through. It had impacted her and she had only been watching from a safe apartment in orbit.

When the rescue happened, the mass of people had been transported into the middle of the big room and they were now spreading out over the large space.

Many stood in front of the large screen showing the planet below. Many just found chairs and sat down, clearly too shocked or tired to even move.

As she walked around, giving orders, helping where she could, she noticed the dark-haired man from the big building often watched her. She was going to have to talk with him at some point.

He and his group were now all back together, and the girl seemed weak, but very happy to see them. Maybe she had decided she wanted to live after all.

Finally, after almost an hour, Gina moved over to the dark-haired man and the group with him from the big stone building. They were all munching on sandwiches and sipping what looked like a fruit drink of some kind. The dark-haired man and the two boys stood, the long-haired man sat and gave comfort to the young girl in the chair beside him.

Gina walked up, smiled, and stuck out her hand to the dark-haired man. "I'm Gina Helm," she said.

He smiled and took her hand. "Benny Slade."

He held her hand just a bit too long and she didn't mind at all. In fact, for a moment she got lost in his dark eyes and smile. And his touch sent shivers through her. She couldn't remember ever feeling like that about meeting anyone else.

When he finally released her hand, she felt a jolt of loss.

Wow, she was really going to have to get a grasp on herself.

Benny introduced her to the professor, the two teen-aged boys, and the young girl named Candice.

"It's very nice meeting you all," Gina said, reverting to her previous way of meeting and talking with survivors. "Is there anything I can get you while we wait to leave orbit?"

"How far are we going out?" the tall boy with red hair asked. She seemed to remember from the introduction that his name was David.

"About two light years," she said. "And we'll wait there until the next pulse passes and then come back. It will take about ten hours total."

"You have faster than light travel?" the other boy asked, clearly excited.

"It's called Trans-tunnel Drive," she said. "Nothing goes faster than light, but that drive bores a hole outside of space and allows long distances to be covered quickly."

"Wow," one of the boys said and she smiled.

This kind of discussion was relaxing her a little. She kept glancing up at Benny and he didn't say a word, just smiled.

"So where have you four been staying?" she asked.

At that question, Benny laughed. "You know the answer to that, don't you, since you found everyone on the island and brought them up here? I assume this is everyone on the island, and in other rooms are survivors from different areas. Right?"

She was stunned. She knew this man was smart from how he had set out to survive, but she didn't realize just how smart, and how calm he was in a situation that had most people just mumbling and afraid.

"You are all in the big stone building," she said, nodding and smiling at him. "And from what I can tell, you are pretty set up for surviving the summer. Well done."

Damn those eyes of his were amazing as he stared at her and nodded.

"So why do you speak English?" the professor asked.

"Actually," she said, "we are all speaking a form of what is called Standard, but when you were transported, we gave you all the ability to understand and speak Standard. It will always sound like we are talking in the same language. But I speak English just fine as well."

"So where exactly are you from?" Benny asked.

She laughed. "Hard to explain."

Benny pointed to the two boys. "I'm sure these two will understand, so give it a try."

She nodded, doing her best to not stare into his eyes too much. "My home world circles a planet in the Lesser Magenelic Cloud."

Both boys reacted at once, excited. "That's a satellite galaxy of the Milky Way," David said to Benny.

"It's a very, very long ways away," the other boy said.

"Are there aliens there?"

She shook her head. "There are no alien civilizations at all in this galaxy or in many others that have been seeded with human life. Only humans like us."

"So this is your real form?" David asked. "Not some sort of image?"

"Everyone on this ship is human," she said, smiling at the young man. "I am very real. The ship is called *Star Conscious* and has a crew of about two thousand, including families, all from human worlds spread over four or five galaxies."

Now even Benny seemed a little shocked, but he said nothing, so she took that as a good moment to move on. Even though she really wanted to stay here, she had a job to do.

"I have to keep moving and checking on everyone," she said. "But I will be back to talk more shortly."

"Looking forward to it," Benny said, smiling a half-smile at her.

Damn, it was everything she could do to just walk away without looking back. Luckily, not more than twenty steps away was another group she hadn't talked to.

And a minute later, when she glanced back, Benny was still watching her as she had watched him the last few days.

Chapter Twenty-one

BENNY HAD no idea how the hundreds of other people in the room felt, but after the little speech by some man in charge, he kept verging on sheer panic that came close to cutting through the trained calm in his head.

He made himself focus on what was happening around him as people spread out, some going for food, others being helped by medical staff, others moving for showers and fresh clothing.

He asked Candice if she needed any medical help and she just shook her head. "Just some food and something to drink."

The professor found her a chair and one for himself after he sent the boys off to get them all something to eat.

In the big room, the five of them were closer to the big window or view screen showing the planet below than most others. After the first few minutes, most everyone had moved more into the big room or to the far walls.

The woman that had shocked him when he saw her with his attraction for her was clearly someone in charge. She was working her way around the room, talking with survivors, getting some of them help, sending someone for food for others.

More than likely, these survivors, probably all from Manhattan, were her responsibility.

And if he had to guess, she had been studying everyone ahead of time. That's how he would set it up if he knew this was coming.

As he watched her, he became more and more attracted to her. She was clearly in shape, strong, and moved like an athlete.

And she was smart, in control, and smiled easily, even under these circumstances.

The boys got back with the food. He took what looked like a roast beef sandwich and a bottle of orange fruit juice that tasted wonderful.

As they ate and he watched the black-haired woman, David asked the professor, "Why the question about the number of survivors?"

"Because there is a magic number of humans that it takes to build a population," the professor said between bites and encouraging Candice to eat slowly. "The human race, at least on this planet, would need population to survive and have a large enough gene pool to make the effort even worthwhile."

"And you know this how?" Benny asked.

"It's my field," he said, smiling. "Or it used to be."

"Is two million enough?" David asked.

The professor laughed. "Far, far more than enough."

Benny figured that at least that was good to hear.

Then, like a shining light in the darkness, the woman with short black hair walked toward them and stuck out her hand, saying her name was Gina Helm.

In all his years, Benny had never felt a touch so electric, a look so attractive as hers.

Up close she was even better looking than she had been from across the room.

Her eyes were a deep green and just seemed to see everything about him.

He flat didn't want to let go of her hand, but managed to and then introduced her to the others.

They talked for a far too short a time before she excused herself to move on. Clearly she had been watching everyone in this room for days ahead, and was the person in charge.

After she moved on to the next group, Benny moved slightly so he could watch her and then asked David a question. "Can you explain to me what she meant when she described where she was from?"

"There are billions of stars in this galaxy, most would have planets," David said.

"But not all would hold human life like Earth," Freddy said, "But at least hundreds of millions would be able to."

"Think of this galaxy like the sun and there are other smaller galaxies circling it like planets," David said.

"She is from one of those other galaxies," Freddy said. "And she said that the crew on this ship is all human from thousands of worlds."

Benny shook his head, not even slightly capable of understanding what the two boys were saying. "So she's from another planet?"

"Yes," David said, "One so far away it's impossible to imagine traveling that distance."

"So she's an alien?" Benny asked.

David and Freddy both shook their heads. "There has always been a theory that humans didn't originate on this planet, that we were seeded by other more advanced humans. That's what she said, so she would be as human as we are."

"Looks human," the professor said, smiling at Benny.

Benny laughed. "That she does."

A voice came over a speaker system, saying simply over the noise. "Everyone is on board safely. We are moving to a safe point now."

David pointed to the window.

Benny pulled his gaze from Gina and turned just in time to see the planet shrink and then vanish in a blur of gray motion.

Maybe ten seconds later the stars returned, with no planet.

"Wow," David said, clearly excited. "It took only a few seconds to move two light years."

Benny had no real idea how far it was they had just traveled. And he honestly wasn't sure if he wanted to know. He had enough to deal with at the moment.

Chapter Twenty-two

GINA MOVED SLOWLY around the room for the next hour, glancing over at Benny at times and once smiling at him and he smiled back.

Now, after almost two hours, the room was settled and her staff had a pretty good control of all the situations.

The room's disinfectant air cleaners had also cleared most of the smells as well, which she was thankful for. In short order, she would be living in that smell of death. She was glad it was gone for the moment now.

Finally, she found herself just standing, looking around. Everything for all the people seemed to be in control.

So she turned and worked her way back toward Benny and the others from the big stone building.

"Looks like the situation is under control," Benny said, smiling at her as she approached. "Nice job."

"Control might be the wrong term," she said, smiling back. "Call it contained panic."

Benny kept smiling and she was drawn even more to him and that wonderful smile that actually reached his eyes. "Been fighting that myself a lot over the last ten days."

"Can't say that I blame you," she said. She looked away from Benny and at the young girl. "You feeling better?"

Candice nodded, but said nothing, just stayed leaning against the professor.

The professor nodded his thanks to her. Clearly he was doing fine as well, taking the responsibility of his last class very seriously. She liked that about him.

"You boys doing all right?" she asked the other two.

Both nodded. "Can't believe we're two light years from Earth."

"It took only seconds," the second one said.

She smiled. "Distance in space between stars is vast. So even at the speed we took this jump, it takes a long time to get some places."

David nodded. "Like to your home world."

"Yes," she said, nodding. "That's a great distance away."

"So what does your home world look like?" Benny asked.

She looked into his eyes and smiled. "Actually, very similar to yours, except that it has a little more land mass and a little less water. But I was born in a city on an island very similar to your Manhattan Island."

All of them nodded and she was about to excuse herself again to keep making

Some Classic Dean Wesley Smith Stories
Available at your favorite booksellers.

rounds when Benny asked a very simple question. "So you sticking around after this rescue operation?"

"I am," she said, figuring it wouldn't hurt to tell him since he would never remember anyway. "Thousands of us will be embedding on your planet to help the recovery along."

"It would be great having you in our building," David said.

Benny smiled at her and nodded.

"I just might take you up on that if you'll have me."

"I think we have more than enough room," the professor said. But he was frowning. She didn't want him to ask the next question. Clearly the professor was very smart as well. No wonder he and Benny had made such a good team getting that big building cleared and set up for survival.

"I've got to go check on everyone else," she said, smiling at the professor and Candice, then at Benny.

His gaze was intense and she had a hunch he also realized something about what she said was wrong.

"Back in a short time," she said, lightly touching his arm as she walked past.

And that simple touch had sent a shock wave through her.

What in the world was going on?

Forcing herself to not look back again at Benny, she started another slow circuit of the big room. She really, really wanted to get to know him. More than anyone she had met before.

But that would happen once she reached the planet.

Nothing that happened here in the next few hours would make a difference because he wouldn't remember it.

Chapter Twenty-three

BENNY WATCHED HER go, wishing he could just walk along with her and talk with her and stay close to her.

Then he glanced down at the professor. "Did something just happen there that I missed?"

Benny had a hunch he knew what it was, but he wanted the professor to confirm his suspicions.

"She's going to come to live in our building," the professor said.

"That is so cool," David said.

"But we won't remember any of this," the professor said, making an assumption that had not yet been stated.

Benny nodded and glanced at where Gina knelt talking with two survivors sitting in chairs.

The professor was right, Benny was sure. He was going to have to meet her all over again.

Part of him was sad about that and part of him was excited that he wouldn't remember any of this.

"We don't ask her that question," Benny said to everyone.

"No point anyway if you are right," David said. "We won't remember the answer."

"But we will meet her again," the professor said. "And even if we don't remember, she's going to be a great help."

Benny couldn't agree more.

Over the next few hours the professor managed to get more food and drink into Candice to make her stronger and want to come back to the building. But through that smell on a hot day was going to be a very nasty hike for her. Benny wasn't sure if she could make it.

But he had a hunch that if Gina showed up, she would work with them to find Candice and others to join the building, and that was exactly what they needed.

She would remember and she would know exactly where everyone was located.

She came by and talked with them twice more in the next few hours and the boys asked her all kinds of science fiction questions. Mostly Benny just listened and enjoyed the time being close to her.

Sometime after nine hours, true to his word, the man who had given the speech at first came back in and everyone got quiet.

"Everyone on the planet, almost two million souls, has survived the second and final wave of deadly electromagnet waves," he said.

The room gave him a cheer and a lot shouted out "Thank you!"

Benny did the same.

And across the room he could see that Gina looked relieved. Benny had no doubt that saving over two million people had to have been a massive undertaking. More than he wanted to imagine.

His style was helping one person at a time.

"We are returning to Earth," the man said, "and will be in Earth orbit in a minute or so."

"So do we have an option of going to another planet?" someone shouted.

"No," the man said, which caused the room to explode in talking.

The man held up his hand for silence and got it. "We will take the extremely wounded and the near-death sick, but all of you, and the two million others on all the ships are the future of humanity on Earth. We can't rob Earth of that."

"How do we survive?" someone shouted from behind where Benny stood.

"Some of you won't," the man said bluntly. "But many will, enough to re-build a wonderful culture and society and preserve much of what is already there. Your job is to save the old art and culture and build new on top of it."

"Wow, the guy is blunt," David said. "And guys, we are back in orbit."

Benny glanced around to see the planet below them.

Suddenly, beside Benny the professor shouted out, "We won't remember any of this, will we?"

The officer smiled. "It is possible, but unlikely," he said. "Most of you won't remember any of this."

That stunned everyone even more than the death sentence he had just declared on many people in the room.

Benny smiled at Gina and pretended to tip his hat at her in thanks.

She smiled back and nodded.

"I wish each and every one of you luck," the man said. "The future of the human race on the planet Earth depends on all of you."

With that a shimmering wave swept over the room.

Benny knew he was going home, to the city he loved, and his new home near the top of the Empire State Building.

Chapter Twenty-four

GINA WATCHED as they all vanished, leaving only her and her team scattered around the room.

Everyone stood in silence for a moment, then turned silently to start cleaning up. Everyone had prepared for this rescue for a long time. It was now over and her job and the others embedding into the culture was just starting.

"Great job," Chairman Carson said to her, stepping down off the stage. He was the captain of this ship. Since every Seeder ship was a business to itself and everyone on board was paid, the captain was called Chairman.

"Thank you," she said. "I'll be starting the next stage tomorrow."

The Chairman nodded, his normally happy face drawn with lines of exhaustion. She hadn't seen him look so tired before.

"We'll cloak in a week or so," he said, "so local sector rescue ships won't know we are remaining here. Get some rest before you start. At this point, the deadline is past, the long slow job of helping rebuild this civilization starts."

"I'm feeling that," she said, nodding. "But also excited to get down there to help and save as many as I can."

He nodded. "Anything you need, don't hesitate."

"Thank you, Chairman."

He transported away, leaving her standing and staring at the mess where over two hundred survivors had been a short time before. The two empty chairs where the professor and Candice had sat seemed hauntingly alone.

She needed to get Candice back to the big building first. Of that she had no doubt.

And she really wanted to meet Benny again, and have time to actually get to know him this time around.

She spent the next hour working with her crew and the medical staff on those injured survivors they had not sent back. There were almost forty of them and she knew they would all be transferred to another ship to be taken to worlds that had volunteered to take them as refugees. Most of the survivors would survive and would get mental help as well as the medical.

Finally, she went back to her apartment, took a long shower, got something to eat, and then went to her screens to check on the people on the island.

No one was moving. It was late afternoon and more than likely the day was hot.

She focused down on the man she had met and was so attracted to. Benny sat in his apartment, alone, his feet up, staring out over the city. He had made a former office into an apartment and it looked very comfortable. He had even set up a nice kitchen with a dining table near a window for the view.

She had no idea what he was thinking about, and she wished she was there to ask him.

Then, as she watched, he did something she couldn't believe he could do.

He stood up, went over to a pad of yellow paper on a counter, then in large script he wrote a note.

As she stared at it, she just shook her head.

The note said:

Gina, please get Candice on your way here tomorrow.

He held that up to the sky for a moment, then put it on the table in plain view.

Then he wrote another note.

I'll set you up an apartment.
There are a lot of people we need to save when you get here.

He put that note on the table beside the first one and then smiled upward before moving over to the chair to sit down again and put his feet up.

He remembered!

Gina just stared at the screen and the slight smile on Benny's face.

How in the hell had he remembered?

How was that even possible?

She just stared at that smile on his handsome face and then just started laughing.

She had some research to do and do quickly.

She teleported to the transportation department of the ship.

Seeders could just teleport from place to place within reason, but every ship also had a transport department for moving others and supplies. And that department had been responsible for the smooth transport of all the survivors who came to this ship. She needed one question answered before she did anything.

She needed to know how Benny could remember.

She needed to know if it was a glitch, or if there was something, as she suspected, very, very special about Benny Slade.

Besides the fact that all she wanted to do was jump him and make love to him.

Chapter Twenty-five

BENNY AWOKE with a slight headache in his big bed. The sun was high in the sky and he glanced at a clock he had put beside the bed. It was after two in the afternoon.

Ten hours.

Then he bolted upright in bed, sitting there, trying to calm his racing heart.

He had had a dream about being taken up to a ship and meeting the most stunning woman he could ever imagine.

In his dream, he had been taken from sleep right before sunrise, about 4:30 a.m. and his dream had him, and everyone, being on the ship for almost ten hours.

He kept staring at the clock.

How was that possible?

He dropped back onto the bed, staring up at the tile in the former office ceiling. They had said no one would remember. Had he imagined it all?

Had he imagined Gina Helm?

He hoped not, but his racing heart wanted to let him believe he had.

He had never given much thought to people living on other planets. The very idea of it had never interested him much at all, actually.

Now it seemed people on a lot of other planets were a very real thing.

Or he had just dreamed it all.

Far more likely.

But not once in his life had he slept for seventeen hours, which was how long it had been since he had crawled into bed.

He lay there in his bed until finally he couldn't stay still any longer.

He had to move, see if there were any answers.

He took a long shower, got into fresh clothes, and headed down to a public area where the professor and the boys spent their time. It was near all their rooms and they all ate lunches and dinners together.

All three of them were sitting there, not talking.

"Anyone have any idea why we all slept so late?" Benny asked, grabbing a cold glass of iced tea and sitting down with them.

"Not a clue," the professor said. "Never slept that long in my entire life."

"We all did," David said. "I think the planet got hit with something again and this time only knocked us out."

Freddy shook his head. "Aliens, I'm sure. They wanted to plant trackers on us or something for their experiments."

Both David and the professor shook their heads.

"It was sure weird," Benny said.

They talked for a few more minutes, then Benny decided to take some action. He had a hunch, if his dream was true, they were going to start having company fairly quickly.

"I'm going to spend the evening setting up a second apartment on my floor. I think because of our lights at night, we need to start getting ready for company pretty soon."

They divided up work, including helping him bring up a second bed, some furniture from an office ten floors down, and another dining table from a lunch room even more floors down. To move furniture, they used the service elevator and he hated it. Even knowing how to get himself out of the elevator didn't help. Having an elevator powered by a generator just wasn't his idea of a confidence builder.

There were two large bathrooms with showers on his floor, so it would easily divide into an apartment for Gina.

He hoped she would want it.

He hoped she was real.

If not, he was going to a lot of work to make a living apartment for a figment of his imagination.

He headed back up to his own apartment after a half hour to sit and do some planning while the professor and the boys did chores and made sure the generators were all working fine, as well as the alarms for the monitors on the doors.

Then after dinner, they would actually set up the new apartment.

It was as he sat looking out over the city that he got the feeling he was being watched.

The windows were tinted to not allow anyone to see in, so he knew it wasn't coming from outside.

The woman of his dreams had tuned in again.

If she was real, and believed he wouldn't remember, she was in for a shock.

He smiled and went over to the table and wrote a couple of notes for her in very large letters.

If she was watching, that would really mess with her mind, and that made him smile even more.

If she wasn't watching, if she didn't really exist, then he hoped one of the survivors they ran across was a good trained counselor, because he was going to need real help for believing in a dream woman from space.

THE FIRST STEPS

Chapter Twenty-six

GINA HAD SPENT a good hour with the fine people in the transport area, trying to understand why anyone from the surface would remember their time on the ship.

She was told there were only two reasons. One was that the equipment had malfunctioned slightly, but she was assured that hadn't happened after they spent a good thirty minutes checking everything over.

The second reason was that the person had the Seeder gene. That tended to sometimes block such things as mind erase. Not all the time, but sometimes, if the person had a very, very strong Seeder gene.

She hadn't known until that moment that there was anything like a Seeder gene. But it seemed there was, and it was a prerequisite to joining the Seeders. It allowed Seeders to comprehend vast amounts of information and not forget any of it over hundreds or even thousands of years of life.

And with the right treatment, it allowed the person to live basically forever, barring accidents. Having that gene allowed the health treatments that stopped all aging and sickness in all Seeders.

So Benny Slade had the Seeder gene.

The idea of that stunned her even more than she wanted to think about.

After her hour with the transportation department, she sent a message to the Chairman that she needed to talk with him.

She wanted to know what was allowed with survivors who remembered the rescue and what wasn't. Not a question ever covered in the training up to this mission, because no one had been expected to remember.

"My office now," was all he responded.

She jumped to his office. It was large, with a number of chairs and a large couch. The walls were a light tan and covered with photos from different planets. There was a large wooden desk with hidden screens that she knew floated over the desk when in use.

She had only been in his office once before and felt she liked Chairman Carson more because of the informal nature of the room.

She was stunned that he had a visitor.

The man with the chairman stood about six feet tall and had long gray hair flowing down his back that he had pulled into a ponytail. He was imposing and striking at the same time. He flat radiated power from his dark eyes.

Chairman Carson was standing in front of his desk talking with the man as she arrived. Carson turned to her. "Gina Helm, I would like you to meet Chairman Wade Ray."

She managed to say, "Nice meeting you."

And then she shook his hand before her tired mind realized that the man she was meeting was one of the most powerful and oldest of all Seeders. No one really knew how old he was. Or even what galaxy he was born in.

What was he doing here?

"Sorry to interrupt," she managed to choke out.

Chairman Ray just smiled. "We were actually talking about you and the great job you did. And about one of the survivors in your area."

Gina managed to get her thoughts back together and said simply, "Benny Slade?"

"You met him I understand," Chairman Ray said, his eyes intense.

"I met him and talked with him a number of times," Gina said, "and found him really amazing and very smart. And I discovered that he did not have his memory wiped by the transport."

"He wouldn't be wiped," Chairman Ray said, and Chairman Carson nodded. "How did you discover this?"

"I checked in on him about an hour ago," she said, "and he must have sensed me watching him and wrote me a note, asked me to pick up another survivor when I arrived in the morning."

"Wow," Chairman Carson said. "And you came here to tell me that?"

Gina shook her head. "Actually, I came here to ask if I could recruit him as a Seeder in this mission. He would be valuable help if I didn't have to hide from him."

Chairman Ray smiled and nodded. "See if you can convince him to join you."

Then Ray turned to Chairman Carson. "Let me know if he does join us."

Chairman Ray then turned to face Gina with those intense eyes of his. "Great job with all this and for discovering Benny Slade's presence in your group. Good luck on the coming mission. I am sure I'll be seeing you soon."

With a slight smile, he vanished.

She stood shocked for a moment, then turned to Chairman Carson. "Can you explain to me what that was all about?"

Carson shrugged and pulled up the image on a screen on his wall of her talking with Benny Slade in the big room. "Somehow he knew about this Benny person and asked about him and your reaction with Benny Slade. So we watched your interaction with Benny and then you asked to see me."

"So why does a survivor on a very damaged planet interest Chairman Ray?" Gina asked, her tired mind swimming in confusion.

Chairman Carson went around the desk and dropped into his big chair and let out a long sigh. "When you figure that out, please let me know as well."

Chapter Twenty-seven

THAT EVENING after dinner, Benny and the professor and the two boys sat up Gina Helm's apartment on the opposite side of the same floor that Benny was on. There were two office doors and a foyer between the two apartments.

Benny didn't tell them who was coming because he was starting to think he imagined it all. But even so, he wanted the apartment to be clean and comfortable.

They moved in a large flat screen and tan living room furniture and a library of old movies. They set up a large bed and turned a small office into a closet with a bench next to where the bed was.

They also managed to move up a fridge and set it up near a sink in a small glassed-in break room, leaving the table and chairs and the dishes in the cabinets. The room already had a small microwave and hot plate, so it would work pretty well, as far as Benny was concerned. Not as nice as his kitchen on the other side of the floor, but good enough.

Then they set up a generator to run on the balcony outside of the apartment, so both of the apartments on the floor could have their own power and air-conditioning.

They got it running to cool down the apartment.

Every so often he got the sense that Gina was watching him and he would glance up and give her the thumbs-up signal. He hoped she would like the place.

And he really hoped she saw his note about picking up Candice on the way here.

Actually, he hoped more than anything that she was real.

After they were done, the professor and the boys went back downstairs to watch a movie. Once again Benny stretched out in his living room, his lights low so he could see out over the darkening city.

There were a few lights scattered over the dark city, but not many.

And he knew people out there could see his lights here as well.

If he hadn't just imagined everything about Gina, very soon they would be recruiting more and more people to join them and help with survival.

And if Gina was real, he had about a thousand questions to ask her, not only about her job and people and space, but about herself.

He really, really wanted to get to know her better.

A lot better.

And never once in his life had he felt that way about a figment of his imagination.

He managed to doze off in his chair after an hour or so and crawl into bed by ten with the alarm set for five a.m. He wanted to be downstairs to greet Gina and Candice.

He had a hunch she would start early, in the coolness of the morning.

That's what he would do.

Chapter Twenty-eight

BENNY WAS JUST crawling out of bed when Gina took one last look at her screens, made sure she had what she needed in her light pack, including water, and informed transport she would be leaving the ship shortly.

She wore jeans and a light white blouse with a sports bra under it. She had on tennis shoes and had three changes of clothes and a pair of running shoes protected from the smell in a sealed bag.

She wore nose filters against the smell for herself and carried a gas mask from the city below for Candice. But she knew that wouldn't begin to stop the odor of walking past and over thousands of dead bodies decomposing in the heat of the streets.

It was not going to be a pretty sight, and she hoped Candice had the stomach for it. If the girl fainted, Gina would transport them both closer to the big stone building that was their destination.

She might have to do that anyway if Candice was passed out. Or if Candice couldn't walk, she would just drug her and transport them both.

Gina did one more double-check of her light provisions. She could transport back to this apartment at any time, but better that she was prepared to stay on the surface as much as possible.

She took a deep breath and then said to herself, "Here we go."

A moment later she found herself in the dim apartment where Candice had been hiding. The decomposing smell of human flesh hit her hard and she forced herself to breathe through her nose to let the filters hold the smell down some.

She moved down the hallway to where Candice had been staying in her bedroom. The girl was curled up under the blankets.

"Candice," Gina said softly. "We need to get out of here and back to the big building with your friends."

"Who are you?" Candice asked weakly, looking up at her.

"I'm just a friend," Gina said. "Come on, let's get you back to the professor and your friends."

"You can take me there?" Candice asked, but didn't move.

"I can," Gina said. She tried to help Candice up, but the young girl just wasn't there. Her arms felt like limp sacks of flesh. There was no doubt to Gina that Candice wasn't going to be able to walk the fifteen blocks to the big stone building.

Especially through all the death.

Gina eased a sedative out of her pack and brushed it over Candice's face as if she was brushing the girl's filthy hair out of her face.

Candice slumped out cold almost instantly.

Gina put the gas mask on Candice's face, then put one arm under the young girl's shoulders and the other under her thighs and lifted her. Candice didn't weigh that much.

Gina then jumped to a spot she knew was blind to Benny's cameras about a half block away from the big stone building and around a corner.

The smell on the street was ten times worse than it had been in the apartment and it made her stagger.

She had imagined this to be bad, but nothing like this.

And the bodies around her were bloated and ugly colors and didn't look anything close to human anymore.

Her stomach threatened to rebel, but she managed to control that by looking up at a wall and focusing on a fire escape there.

Then she forced herself to breathe only through her nose, but the smell made her eyes water and she wanted to just stop and throw up.

She moved around the corner so Benny's security cameras could see her and then leaned against the side of a building for a moment, still holding Candice in her arms.

The feel of the solid stone building wall gave her strength.

This was going to be so much harder than she had ever imagined.

After a moment she started forward, making sure to walk mostly in the street around the cars because that was far, far easier than walking around the bodies she didn't want to look at on the sidewalk.

When she was within a hundred paces of the main door to the big stone building, it flew open and both Benny and the professor came charging out, moving as fast as they could into the street.

"Got her," Benny said, smiling at Gina and taking Candice.

The professor moved around and supported Gina and the four of them headed into the building.

"I'm fine," Gina said. "And I think she is as well. She just fainted."

"Professor, get the doors locked back up and the alarms reset," Benny said. "We'll take her to the floor below yours for cleanup and such."

Benny got onto an elevator carrying Candice and Gina followed.

"Glad I wasn't dreaming," Benny said as the door closed and they started up.

Gina smiled at him. "Glad you weren't either."

Then all the way up they just stared at each other, smiling like kids on a first date.

Chapter Twenty-nine

ON THE EXCUSE of looking at their security set-up, Benny had the professor go down to the lower levels with him. Benny had a hunch that if he hadn't imagined Gina, and she had seen his note, she and Candice would be arriving in the next half hour or so, before the sun really climbed into the sky and started to heat up the mess outside once again.

The lower levels had a faint smell of rotting death, but the solid building was holding most of it out. But Benny had no doubt it was going to be a long, hot, stinking summer.

As Benny and the professor reached the security room, an alarm sounded and there, on the screen, Gina staggered around the edge of a building about a block from their main doors and leaned against a wall.

She was real!

Spaceships and rescues and millions of survivors were all real.

Holy shit! How was that possible?

But it was.

He just stared at the screen, his mouth open, every muscle in his body frozen.

Gina Helm, a human from a very great distance away, stood there on the corner with Candice in her arms.

Gina had the exact same short black hair that he remembered, and the trim body now dressed in jeans and a light blouse. She looked just as she did on the spaceship in orbit.

She was real!

It had not been a dream.

Gina rested for a moment against the building, then went into the street and started toward the main door, seemingly carrying Candice without much of a problem.

"That's Candice!" the professor shouted.

That shocked Benny into movement and the two of them took off running down the two flights of stairs and to the front door. Benny got it open and they both ran out into the intense stink of the street as Gina got close.

He smiled at Gina, not at all believing his eyes.

Then he took Candice from Gina's arms.

Candice was so light, it shocked him.

As the professor locked up, he and Gina took Candice up the elevator to the floor under where the professor and the boys lived. It had once been a number of small offices, each with bathrooms. The room had a large main area just off the elevators. They had set up that floor with showers, trash disposal for clothes that could not be salvaged from the smell, and soaking sinks near some wash machines for the clothing that could be saved.

They had also brought in about forty bathrobes of all sizes and had them hanging around the area. No one was allowed onto the living floors smelling like the death in the streets. That was the rule of the building and an important one.

He put Candice on a tabletop near the center of the big area and checked her vitals. She seemed to just be sleeping.

"I had to knock her out with a light sedative," Gina said. "She should be fine in a few hours and some food."

"Good," Benny said. "Very glad you saw my note."

"And that note was very good thinking on your part," she said. "It forced me to research and learn a lot about why you could remember the ship."

"I'm interested in hearing about that," Benny said, smiling at her.

As the elevator dinged and the professor came bounding into the room, Gina turned and introduced herself, using the same name she had used on the ship.

Benny figured that was her real name, but he would ask later to make sure.

She told the professor she had seen Candice trying to make her way here and just helped her. Benny nodded to her in agreement of her cover story as she turned back.

"You have showers here?" Gina asked, looking around.

Benny showed her the set-up of the different offices, all with bathrooms and installed showers that they had put in, while the professor stayed close to Candice.

"You bring a change of clothes?" Benny asked her.

"Got some in sealed bags in my pack," she said. "And my pack can be wiped down and won't absorb odors. How about I get myself and Candice showered and cleaned up and into fresh clothes? What do I do with her old clothes?

Benny showed her the black bags to wrap them up in and where to throw them down an elevator shaft they had blocked open.

He was stunned at how calm she was acting and sounding. His heart was racing a mile a minute and it was everything he could do to stay calm.

The attraction he felt for her was more now than it had been on the ship.

"You should be able to save your clothes," he said. "Toss them in a sink for them to soak and I'll show you how to wash them later."

"Thank you," she said, nodding.

Then she looked into his eyes and both of them sort of froze.

Finally he managed to say, "We have a lot of talking to do later."

"With that I agree," she said, smiling at him and making the breath in his throat catch. "About more than you can ever imagine."

Chapter Thirty

GINA WAITED with Candice while Benny and the professor took showers, changed clothes, and tossed their other clothes into some hot water to soak. Then they headed upstairs, leaving her to help the young girl.

She was stunned at how handsome Benny was coming out of that room with fresh clothes and wet hair. She just wanted to touch him. And that was so out of character for her.

"We'll be at the top of that flight of stairs if you need help with Candice," Benny said as they left.

"I'll manage fine and bring her up with me," Gina said.

Then she stripped Candice and tossed her clothes away. Then Gina took off her clothes as well and put them in a sink full of water next to Benny's clothes to soak.

Then she picked up Candice and carried her to a shower in a side office.

Candice didn't wake up, which was fine. Gina got both of them scrubbed down and both of their hair cleaned. She used some of the special chemicals she had brought from the ship to neutralize the odor. She dried them both off and got Candice in underwear and a bathrobe.

Then Gina pulled out one of her extra pair of clothes, took her nose plug filters out, and stored them in her pack, and got dressed.

Then she wiped her pack down and put it over her shoulder.

"Time to go the final steps to home," she said to Candice as she picked her up.

The young girl was so light, it was scary. She carried Candice up the flight of stairs without a problem.

It felt good to actually be rescuing someone from certain death. She knew that they had rescued everyone on the planet, but that had only been for a few hours.

This rescue of Candice, Gina hoped, would last, and that Candice would help rebuild this new world. All over the planet a thousand Seeders were doing the same thing, trying to help one person at a time to survive.

When she reached the next floor, Benny, the professor, and the two young men were there.

Benny quickly took Candice from Gina and got the young girl into a bed in a private room off to one side of the main room.

The professor had fixed some soup and had some crackers. The two boys just hovered close by, looking relieved and worried for their friend.

After Benny got Candice tucked in, he came out. "Take turns sitting with her and get her food and water when she wakes up," he said to the professor and the boys.

Gina then introduced herself to the two boys and both of them thanked her for bringing Candice.

After a short time, Benny said in front of everyone, "We have an apartment you might like that we just finished, if you are interested in staying with us for a while."

He smiled at her and she nodded. "I think I would like that. There are a lot of things I can do to help out."

"We'll talk about that tonight over dinner," Benny said, smiling at her.

Damn that smile of his could melt an iceberg. And she was far, far from being an iceberg.

She and Benny climbed up the flights of stairs so he could show her the apartment they had set up for her. They didn't really talk. She wasn't sure what exactly to say yet. It slightly annoyed her that she was acting like a school girl with a crush on a guy, but everything about Benny affected her and she had no idea why.

But she liked the feeling of really being attracted to someone. It had been a long time since that had happened and never this strong on first sight that she could remember.

She left her pack in her new bedroom. She was going to like staying here. The apartment, even being put together from what had clearly been an office area, was comfortable and the view was something to behold.

The windows in her living room showed an amazing city stretching far beyond the limits of the water on either side of the island. What had happened to this planet was one of the great tragedies of the galaxy. Of that she had no doubt.

She walked slowly around, looking at all the details Benny had set up for her as he quickly described it all. Granted, she had watched them set up this apartment, but actually being in it felt different.

It felt right.

"This is wonderful," she said after Benny was done with the short tour. "It seems perfect."

She smiled at him and he just looked into her eyes for a long moment.

"Thanks," he said, finally. "Not as good as your place on the ship, I bet."

"In some ways," she said, "I think it's better."

She wanted to add that it was better because he was close by, but she didn't. She was amazingly attracted to this man, but she really didn't know him at all. They both had so much to learn about each other.

She had to be careful, not move too fast, even though she wanted to.

Actually, what she wanted more than anything was to just kiss him and pull him to that freshly made bed.

But she managed to remain in control.

And she had no idea how she was going to tell him about the Seeder part of things.

"How about we go down and check on the professor and the boys and Candice," Benny said after a moment of silence. "Grab a little lunch, then bring it back up here and talk."

"That sounds perfect," she said.

And it did.

Chapter Thirty-one

BENNY CHECKED on Candice, who still seemed to be sleeping comfortably. The professor and the boys were not going to be far from her. He hadn't realized how much her disappearance had really bothered them until Candice showed up on the ship.

Now it seemed her appearance had given them new life. They had set up a chair just inside her open bedroom door so someone would be there when she woke up.

When he came out, the professor and David were sitting at the big oak meeting table they used to eat meals and Freddy was sitting just inside Candice's door listening to their conversation.

Gina was standing, leaning against a counter so she could face everyone. And it felt wonderful to have her here and part of this group.

It actually felt natural, which was odd considering she had only been here an hour or so at most.

He dug out of the fridge the fixings for sandwiches and started to put them together.

"I think we need to be getting a few more floors ready for more guests," he said as he worked. He was using some of the last thinly-sliced roast beef from the deli that they had kept in the freezer. He was going to miss deli roast beef more than he wanted to think about.

And bread. He and the professor had talked at one point about trying to figure out how to make bread and grow vegetables and other things, but at the moment, with canned food and other things that didn't spoil quickly, they had more than enough to make it for a year or so. It just wasn't going to be a varied diet, but it would keep them alive.

"How many people are you set up for now?" Gina asked.

"We could hold fifty, maybe," the professor said and Benny nodded his agreement. "We're ready for that now."

But with fifty, Benny knew that would make it critical to go out regularly searching for more food.

"That's a pretty good number," Gina said, nodding.

From what Benny could tell, she was impressed.

David and the professor then asked Gina some basic questions and she had told them she had been in the subway when everything happened, had holed up

Now Available

from all your favorite booksellers
in trade paper and electronic editions.

down there for a time, but decided she didn't like that and it felt dangerous. Plus she said it smelled bad down there, with the moisture and all. So she came up to see if she could find anyone alive.

Benny had just listened to her cover story, nodding. It was sound and had no places for any real questions.

"Where you from originally?" the professor asked.

"My family moved around a lot," she said. "And I just kept on moving when I got older. So nowhere, really. But I sure love New York."

Benny smiled and nodded. Again a great cover story that didn't pin her to any one place. There was absolutely nothing at all suspicious about her story and if he didn't remember meeting her on a huge spaceship in orbit, he would have been completely buying the story as well.

"You can see your lights from all over the city," Gina said. "So as more discover they are not in a good place, they will try to get here, I'm sure. So I agree with Benny that setting up more living quarters would be a good idea. But fifty is a great start."

"You think we should track some of their lights as well and try to offer them a room here?" the professor asked.

"I don't think it would hurt," Benny said, putting the sandwiches in front of everyone and handing Gina a plate. Then he took Freddy a plate with a sandwich on it and a small bag of potato chips.

The professor nodded. "I agree. After Candice wakes up, I'll start really looking at more spaces in the building we could convert easily."

Benny nodded. "Gina and I will be upstairs. I want her to fill me in on what she's seen around the city. Let us know when Candice wakes."

"We will," the professor said, nodding.

When they got into the stairwell and started the climb, both carrying their plates of food, Gina looked over at Benny. "Those are some very good people you have there."

"I know," he said. "And all three of them are as smart as a whip."

She laughed. "Never heard that expression before."

"I'm not surprised," Benny said. "It's an old one."

And he wasn't surprised. No way anyone just studying the planet could learn all the language. So he figured that the walk up the stairs was as good a time as any to ask the first of what he figured would be a thousand or more questions.

"How long did you have to study this planet, anyway?"

"Basic preparations I did on the way here three weeks ago," she said. "But almost all of what I studied was in the last ten days."

"Wow, you really didn't have any time, did you?"

She sighed beside him and he looked over at her pained face.

"I think if the powers that be out there in the big universe had learned of this tragedy sooner," she said, softly, "they would have saved a lot more people than just the two million from the last wave."

She was actually pained by what had happened here. This planet, this city, wasn't just her job. These were real people to her and to those she worked for.

That was very clear.

And at that moment he realized just how important saving lives was to Gina and her people. And that eased about a thousand of his fears.

There were still a few thousand more he could think of, but his feelings for her eased a lot of them as well.

Chapter Thirty-two

GINA COULDN'T REMEMBER when she enjoyed a lunch more than that first one with Benny. They sat at his table in his apartment near the windows looking out over the city. The air-conditioning was running softly in the background and she could faintly hear the generator on the balcony outside.

The city spread out around them still looked fresh and almost alive. From where they were, they couldn't see any of the streets and that was fine with her. She didn't need a constant reminder of what was below them.

They talked about everything as they ate, from Benny's degrees in college, which didn't really surprise her that he was that smart, to her home planet and how she had grown up and been recruited into the Seeders.

And the sandwich had been amazing. She ended up devouring it and then telling him how much she liked it.

"Don't get used to it," he said, looking sad. "Not a lot of that beef left and there won't be more for a very long time."

She only nodded to that.

He finished his sandwich and pushed his plate away, then leaned back. "Shall we get to some of the hard questions we've both been avoiding?"

She laughed and he just smiled. Damn he was smart and she loved that about him.

And that look in his eye told her that he loved when she laughed as well.

"So ask away," she said. "I promise I'll tell you the truth no matter what."

He nodded. "The boys seemed to be stunned at how far away your home world is. How long did it take you to get here?"

"I didn't come from my home world directly here," she said. "I was working on another planet in this area of this galaxy, so the trip didn't take that long. A week or so to get into position. But if I was on a fast ship directly from my home world to here, it would take about a half year."

He nodded to that and seemed to file it away.

"Explain to me how humans have spread so far in space? I remember a little of what you said on the ship, but my attention was elsewhere."

"Fair enough," she said, taking a sip of a soda and then sitting back so she could look at him directly.

"A very long time ago," she said, "from a planet so distant from here that no one I know of even knows where it might be, the first humans evolved and jumped into space."

"How long ago?" he asked.

She shrugged. "Some say only hundreds of thousands of years ago, others say millions and millions of years ago. I tend to go to the millions of years ago number."

He nodded. "Can't say I understand that kind of number, but go on."

"After the first humans spread out to the stars, they discovered that they were alone. There are no alien cultures out there that anyone knows about. None in this galaxy, my galaxy, or any galaxy close to here."

"So humans really are alone in the cosmos," he said.

"As far as anyone has found so far, yes," she said. Then she went on. "Those early humans figured out a way to seed humanity on planets that could support life. They also seeded all plant and animal life from the original first human home, so every planet with humans on it has the same plants and animals around them."

"Wow, that's a job," Benny said, shaking his head.

"It is," she said. "The Seeders, as we are called, are very good at this now after all this time."

"So you help with this seeding?" Benny asked.

"No," she said. "The front line of the seeding ships has already left this galaxy. They are working in the Andromeda galaxy. My job as a Seeder is to help the cultures start to mature. I get involved in one fashion or another in the growing cultures to help them get past certain disaster points and grow. I embed in cultures, as I am doing now, to help with what I can help with."

"How often have you done that?" he asked.

She took a deep breath. This was the first major problem point and from here on out she might lose this man. And that scared her to death.

"I promised I would tell you the complete truth, remember?" she said.

He nodded, looking very serious.

"This is my tenth time embedding in a culture on ten different planets."

A frown crossed his face. "So tell me what you are worried about in how that is possible for you to do that and still look as good as you do."

She smiled at that and nodded. "Thank you."

"Just truth," he said, smiling at her and her stomach twisted even harder. She was deathly afraid she was about to have Benny start hating her.

"I like this feeling between us," she said. "And I don't want to lose that, so I'm afraid of telling you a lot of this."

"Trust me to deal with what you are saying," he said.

She nodded.

"Seeders are picked to be sort of the guiding hands of cultures for thousands of years as they grow and develop and jump into space. We do not get sick, nor do we age, and we have memories that can remember just about anything. We can also do this."

She teleported to a place thirty steps from him and he damn near went over backwards.

She teleported back into her chair.

She had to show him that she wasn't a normal woman and that was one of the quickest ways she could think to do it.

"That's got to come in real handy," he said, his voice only cracking once as he adjusted his chair.

"So to answer your question truthfully and directly," she said. "I was born just over 200 years ago. And there is no upper limit on how long I can live barring accidents. I have heard of some Seeders being thousands of years old. Maybe older for all I know."

He sat there staring at her for the longest time while her heart almost beat out of her chest with worry. Then he said, "You look damn good for an old broad."

For a moment she didn't completely understand, then he smiled slightly and she laughed.

"Well, thank you," she said. "I guess."

He looked hard at her and then said, "Why do I get the sense you aren't telling me something really important."

She leaned forward and reached her hand across the table, offering it to Benny.

After a moment's hesitation, he took it.

She could feel the incredible attraction of the man pulling at her. His strong, work-worn hand rested in her hand and she kept her gaze locked on his dark, intense eyes.

"The reason you remember the ship," she said, "is because you have the Seeder gene as well. You could be a Seeder as well if you wanted."

He actually jerked at that, but didn't let go of her hand.

She squeezed his hand and then sat back, pulling away from touching him so he could just think.

"Besides living a long time," he said after a moment, "what does being a Seeder really mean?"

"It means that your life mission becomes to help all humans and humanity," she said, "no matter what planet they are on."

"And how many planets is that?" he asked.

"Do you have any idea how many people were in this city before the disaster?" she asked.

"Millions and millions," he said, "if you count all the boroughs across the rivers."

"There are more seeded human planets in just this galaxy than humans who used to be in this city."

"Oh," was all he said.

She let him sit in silence. At least he wasn't storming off. She wasn't sure what she would have been doing if the situations were reversed.

"And how many Seeders are there?" he asked.

"Not enough," she said. "Never enough, which is why I hope you'll join us."

"I'm not much of a joiner," he said.

"You don't join Seeders like joining some lodge," she said. "This is all a job and we all get paid for it."

"You get paid for helping people and living a long time?" he asked, looking directly at her.

"I do," she said, nodding. "And to be honest, I can't imagine a better job."

He nodded to that and sat back.

She just sat there, trying not to hold her breath in worry.

Finally he spoke again. "And after all this time you aren't married or have a boyfriend?"

"Never married," she said, "but I had some boyfriends along the way, but never one that was a Seeder, so I always had to leave them after a decade or so."

"Because you didn't age," he said.

She nodded. "And my job moved me on. So no, I have no boyfriend now."

"And you are telling me the complete truth on everything?" he asked.

"I am," she said.

He looked at her. "So tell me the truth on this question. Are you attracted to me?"

She laughed and then stared him right in the eye. "More than I want to let myself believe. It's every damn thing I can do to not drag you into that bedroom."

"Oh, great," he said, smiling at her. "A woman with self-restraint."

Chapter Thirty-three

HE HAD ENJOYED the lunch and the conversation with Gina more than he wanted to admit. She was smart and attractive and funny.

And clearly she was attracted to him as much as he was to her.

127

But then when she started really telling him about herself, including how old she really was, he felt just stunned.

And when she just vanished from her chair and appeared across the room, then appeared back in her chair, he had damn near gone over backwards.

He wasn't sure what he had been expecting from a woman from space, but that had shocked him.

And her age, for a moment had shocked him as well.

But what had shocked him more than anything was her telling him that he had a special gene that allowed him to join her organization if he wanted. And that was why he had remembered her and the spaceship.

He really didn't understand everything she had told him. But he did understand when she said she could barely keep from taking him into the bedroom.

That he liked and understood completely, because he felt the same way about her.

After she said that he stood, indicating that she should remain where she was.

He moved over to the stairway door and bolted it closed as she watched.

Then he came back over to her and took her hand and helped her to her feet.

Then he kissed her.

For an instant she seemed shocked, then she melted against him, her perfect body pushing into his as her lips matched his.

He had kissed his share of women over the years, but that felt like a combination of a first kiss with a first girlfriend and kissing someone who he had kissed forever.

It was both perfect and exciting at the same time.

They fit together.

The kiss seemed to last for a very long time, then finally he pulled back and she looked at him. They were both almost the same height, so she looked him right in the eye, which he liked.

Her face was red and flushed and he had a hunch his was as well.

"Sorry," he said, smiling, "I just don't have as much self-restraint as you do."

She laughed, then said, "Well, you killed mine with that kiss, that's for sure."

With that, she took his hand and led the way into his bedroom. She kissed him again as they stood beside the bed. Then she pushed back and started unbuttoning her shirt.

He stood there, staring, more than likely his mouth open.

She pulled off her shirt and tossed it to one side, leaving her in jeans and a sports bra.

Wow.

She smiled at him. "You're falling behind."

Then she unzipped her jeans and slid them down over her hips, showing him her black panties.

She had to be the most attractive and in-shape woman he had ever seen or met.

He pulled his shirt over his head and tossed it to one side, then took off his pants as well as she slipped her sports bra over her head and then took off her underwear, exposing a small area of dark hair.

He took his pants off, showing her that he was about as aroused as a man could get.

She stared at him for a moment, then went into his arms, putting his penis between her legs and kissing him, pressing against him.

And he kissed back.

He pushed back into her strong arms, enjoying the feel of her breasts smashed into his chest, her legs holding his penis.

Finally, he pulled away, picked her up and put her on the bed.

She pulled him down on top of her and he was inside her.

Then he lost all track of time and emotions and everything as he made love to the woman of his dreams.

Chapter Thirty-four

GINA LAY WRAPPED in Benny's strong arms, her head on his shoulder, her right leg over him.

She was still breathing hard and trembling from the number of orgasms she had had.

Benny's chest was raising and falling as he too worked to recover. His skin felt hot and wonderful to her.

Everything about this man felt right.

And making love to him had felt perfect, as if they belonged together.

One part of her mind wondered how that was even possible while another part didn't care. She just wanted to enjoy being with him more and more.

She pressed against him, not wanting to move.

"It seems," he said, "that when we're together, self-restraint might be a problem."

She laughed. "Trust me, what we just did will never be a problem for me."

"Me either," he said, turning his head to her and kissing her again, just long enough to make it clear he cared, but not long enough to get things started again.

"I got to ask another question," he said, staring up at the ceiling. "A serious one."

"Go ahead," she said.

"If I joined on to being a Seeder," he said, "would we leave here?"

"No," she said. "When I discovered you had the Seeder gene, I asked Chairman Carson if I could recruit you to help. I figure the two of us here could get a lot more done together than if I was trying to hide from you."

"Chairman Carson?" Benny asked.

"The man who gave the speech on the ship. Seeder ships, and most human spaceships from other planets, are all businesses. And everyone on board is hired to do a job. So instead of having captains, the person who runs a Seeder ship is called a chairman."

"As in chairman of the board?" Benny asked.

"Exactly," she said.

"So we would remain here, helping here, working together?" Benny asked.

"We would," she said.

"And how would you feel about that?" he asked.

She pushed her naked body into his and kissed his cheek.

"Besides the sex," he said, trying not to laugh.

She stopped and chuckled. "Honestly, I think we could be a fantastic team and help a lot more people together than we ever could apart. And I like the idea of working with you a great deal."

"Seriously?" he asked.

"Seriously," she said. "Right from the first moment I saw you, I had a hunch we would be a good team. And I hoped beyond hope that you learning about me and Seeders wouldn't mess all that up. It didn't, did it?"

He could hear the worry suddenly in her voice. And that relaxed him even more.

"I got a lot of things to figure out," he said, turning and kissing her. Then he said, "But wanting to work with you isn't one of those things."

"Good," she said, kissing him again, this time with more passion.

She could feel his penis starting to stir again under her leg and she liked the idea of that.

"Hold on," he said, pulling back from the kiss. "One more question. Is there an easy way for me to learn all about Seeders? Some sort of brain meld or something?"

She laughed. "We have high-speed education systems that can help you learn something quickly, if that's what you mean."

"Perfect," he said. "I want to do that so I really understand before I agree to anything."

"Very smart thinking," she said.

Then he kissed her again and pulled her over on top of him.

A moment later he was back inside of her and time ended and all the problems she faced flew away for her for the moment as all she wanted to make love to this fantastic man.

And she did.

For longer than she ever thought possible.

Chapter Thirty-five

JUST OVER AN HOUR later, they had managed to get untangled and get dressed and head down the stairs for some dinner. Outside the windows, the sun was still pretty high in the evening sky and he could tell it was a hot day out there.

Thankfully, with the two generators running air-conditioning, the floor had stayed cool.

Benny felt stunned at how good it had felt to make love to Gina. Perfect in more ways than he could even imagine.

And her body was stunning. Her skin was smooth, her hair soft, her muscles hard and firm. He doubted she had an

Some Classic Jukebox Stories
Available at your favorite booksellers.

extra ounce of fat on her. He would have to ask her later what she did for exercise. He had brought up to his floor a treadmill and some free weights, and he figured on decent days, he could run around the observation balcony a few floors up.

If he had ever thought to imagine his perfect woman, he wouldn't have done that good a job in his imagination to even come close to Gina in reality.

She only had a few problems. She was from space and she was two hundred years old. But he was fairly certain he could deal with both of those.

They walked down the stairs hand-in-hand, like two kids on a first date, which he guessed this actually was.

Then just outside the door to the floor where the professor and the three kids lived, he turned and kissed her again.

"What's that for?" she asked, smiling at him.

"Because it feels good," he said, grinning like a kid in high school at her.

She kissed him then.

"What was that for?" he asked when she pulled away.

"Because it feels good and a promise for more later."

"Now that I like," he said.

He turned and pulled the stairway door open.

The professor and David were working on dinner at the kitchen counter they had moved in from a nearby furniture store. Freddy and Candice were sitting at the big wooden conference table they used as a kitchen table.

Candice was dressed in a blue blouse and jeans and she had her blonde hair combed and pulled back. She smiled at him when they entered.

He couldn't believe how really thrilled it made him feel to see Candice sitting there like that.

"Wow," Benny said, smiling back at Candice. "Wonderful to see you feeling better."

"Exhausted still," Candice said, "but I needed to get up and move around again."

Some More Classic Jukebox Stories
Available at your favorite booksellers.

Benny indicated Gina and introduced her.

"Thank you," Candice said, smiling at Gina. "The professor tells me you were carrying me here. I don't remember at all, other than thinking a beautiful angel had come to rescue me."

Benny agreed with both the beautiful and the angel part.

"You are more than welcome," Gina said. "And trust me, I'm really glad we met. You were the one that directed me here to this wonderful place and these great people. So I need to thank you for saving me."

Benny smiled at that fib. It was a perfect one. Gina really had a great way with making people feel right about themselves.

"I did?" Candice asked, looking surprised.

"When I met you on the street," Gina said, "you mumbled something about needing to get to the Empire State Building and then collapsed. So I brought you here."

Candice shook her head. "I don't remember any of that. But thank you for getting me here and getting me cleaned up."

"You would have done the same for me," Gina said, sitting down at the table across from Candice.

Benny took the seat across from Gina and nodded.

Candice was smiling, clearly feeling better. Benny figured that with one small lie, Gina just might have saved a life.

"So you like the apartment we set up?" Freddy asked.

"I do," Gina said, her voice enthusiastic. "It's wonderful. Thank you all for allowing me to stay here. I promise I'll carry my weight."

"Before you two came in," Candice said, "we were talking about how Benny thinks there will be more people joining us. Do you think so as well?"

"I do," Gina said. "That's part of what Benny and I were talking about upstairs."

Benny nodded, really, really appreciating how smooth Gina was. "She has information about where some other groups are located, and where some single people are holed up."

"Some will see our lights," the professor said. "Others, I think we need to go talk to."

"I agree," Benny said. Then he looked at Gina. "Can you tell us which ones you met that might be good candidates for this building and if they would want to come here?"

"I met some of them," she said, nodding, "and saw a lot of lights at night after the power went out. I think I can find them again."

"This building is clearly large enough for more people," the professor said.

Benny couldn't agree more. And from what he remembered of some of those people while they were all in the spaceship, they needed a better place to stay and some of them would need help and a direction and a feeling there might be a future to just survive.

Gina changed the subject by asking Freddy what he had been studying in school.

Benny watched her be sociable, smiling easily, keeping the mood light and the questions away from the tragedy.

He flat wanted to spend a lot of time with her. As much as possible, actually. He knew that without a doubt.

Tonight, after dinner, Benny would ask Gina what benefits there would be for him being a Seeder as well in the coming years. If being able to jump around from place to place like she did was one of the things he would learn to do, that would be enough.

And a chance to be with her for a long time would be even more worth it.

Chapter Thirty-six

GINA ENJOYED her dinner with the professor, his three charges, and Benny. The conversation was light and about survival. She knew that all of them had a lot of trauma to get through, but with time they would work through it.

And Gina had decided about halfway through dinner that she would help Candice. The girl had a real brain and if she could get past the next few weeks, she would be a real asset to the future of this planet.

After dinner, all of them showed Gina the other floors they had set up for more survivors. Each floor had once been offices, but now were set up to handle five or six people living comfortably in lots of room. Each floor had a number of bathrooms, had private bedrooms for everyone, and a community living area with kitchen and couches and big screens for movies.

They had done the work on eight different floors. Gina was flat impressed.

Then they went down a few more floors to offices that had not been set up.

"We have room here and in the three floors below this one for more people. Each floor would hold six or seven more people."

"I honestly don't want to go back out into that smell right now," Candice said.

Gina moved over and put her arm around the young girl. "I have a hunch we can wait until things calm into the fall before worrying about these rooms."

"I agree," Benny said. "Candice, I don't see you needing to go back out there anytime soon, to be honest with you."

"Thank you," she said softly.

Gina kept her arm around the young girl and together they went to an elevator.

"Working on a generator?" Gina asked.

"Starts up when the button is pushed," Benny said. "And only this one elevator works. As we go up I'll tell you how to get out of one if it stops or gets stuck."

"Thank you," Gina said, suddenly realizing she hadn't even given that any thought since she could teleport anywhere if she needed to.

When they got back to the main floor, Gina asked Candice how she was doing.

"Tired," Candice said.

Gina led the young girl into her bedroom and closed the door behind her.

Candice dropped on the bed. "I'm so glad I'm back here."

"I think everyone is glad you are as well," Gina said, smiling, "in case you can't tell."

"I can," she said, her voice quivering a little. "They are my new family, aren't they?"

"They are," Gina said. "And you couldn't ask for a better group. We all are family now, and we all have to work together."

Candice nodded, clearly getting more tired by the moment.

"Crawl in and get some sleep," Gina said. You are safe here. And if you need something, I'll be here. Us girls got to stick together, you know."

Candice smiled at that and nodded. "Thank you for carrying me here."

"Thank you for getting me to this wonderful group of people," Gina said.

Then she stood and headed for the door. "Sleep well."

"I think tonight I will," Candice said.

Gina went back out into the main area and pulled the door closed behind her.

Benny was cooking something in the kitchen and he glanced up at her and she nodded.

She could hear the professor and the two boys talking in the living room area about movies. Benny was working on making them some popcorn.

"She going to be all right?" Benny asked, indicating Candice's room.

"I think she might be now," Gina said, moving over and leaning against a counter so she could see Benny.

"Great work with her," Benny said.

Gina nodded. "She's going to have some rough patches, as everyone will. The key is for us to help them through the bad times as much as possible."

Benny glanced over at the living room area to make sure he couldn't be heard, then turned back to her. "Knowing there is a larger world out there and that we are getting support helps me more than I can tell you."

She nodded. "Too bad we can't tell everyone, but most would not believe it and many it would hurt instead of help."

"Found that out the hard way, huh?"

"On a lot of different worlds in a lot of different ways," she said. "It was why I had to have permission to even talk with you, even though you remembered the ship."

"Makes sense," he said as the wonderful-smelling popcorn started to pop.

"Are we joining them for a movie?" she asked.

He smiled at her. "I was kind of hoping you could give me a quick lesson on the Seeders."

She felt a huge feeling of relief wash over her. "That I would be glad to do."

"Then if we feel up for it, we can watch a movie and have popcorn upstairs."

"Perfect," she said. "Just perfect."

FORMING A TEAM

Chapter Thirty-seven

AFTER THEY DELIVERED the popcorn to the guys in the living room, Benny both said goodnight to them and Gina thanked them again for allowing her in their building. Then they headed for the staircase. The sun was just setting to the west, the sky a beautiful orange with the sunset.

A few lights were shining through the dark city, but very few. Benny felt they needed to get out there, start trying to help people, but he was going to need to depend on Gina to guide them in the best way of doing that.

And who to even approach without getting shot on sight.

"You ready to get some information," Gina asked as they closed the door to the apartment and stopped on the landing outside the door.

"We need to lock up this staircase door at our floor," Benny said, suddenly realizing what she was intending. "Just in case someone comes up to find us for some reason or another."

"Good thinking," she said.

An instant later they were inside the door on their floor.

It took him a second to get his bearings, but not long.

"Wow," Benny said. "I could get used to doing that."

"Can't ever let anyone see you do it, though," she said.

He showed her how to lock up, then turned to her.

His stomach was doing flip-flops and he had a hunch he was sweating slightly.

"You trust me?" she asked.

"I do," he said. "But keep in mind all this space stuff is not anything I ever once thought about before meeting you."

She stepped up and kissed him hard. Then she stepped back and looked at him.

He honestly had to admit her kiss calmed him some, in some ways, and excited him in others.

"I honestly do remember what that feels like," she said. "I was twenty-eight, working with relief groups on a major flooding disaster on my planet. My planet had been in space for a hundred years or so, but I sure never thought of going. My job was in the mud helping people survive and rebuild."

"Recruited?" Benny asked.

She nodded. "One of the women working beside me asked me if I would be interested in helping out on a much larger scale. I said sure. But let me tell you, I didn't handle learning about Seeders anyway near as well as you are."

"Oh, I'm screaming and running in my mind," Benny said. "Just never learned how to do that in real life."

"Lucky for me," she said, kissing him.

She turned to the air. "Captain Carson, Benny Slade and I would like to talk with you for a moment."

She nodded. "Thank you, chairman."

Then Benny watched as she said into thin air, "Two transporting aboard."

She nodded a moment later and turned to Benny. "Here we go."

The next moment they were standing in the same position in a large office.

The place had a few soft chairs, a tan couch, and a huge wooden desk. The carpet under Benny's feet was soft and the air smelled fresh.

Pictures of children hung on one wall, while the other white walls were decorated in photos of beautiful scenes of waterfalls and sand dunes.

The man who had spoken to everyone in the big room was coming around the desk, his hand out, smiling.

Benny shook his hand.

"Chairman Carson, this is Benny Slade," Gina said.

"Great meeting you," the chairman said, shaking Benny's hand with a firm handshake.

The man had dark eyes and the smile on his face was also in his eyes.

"Great meeting you as well, sir," Benny said.

"No sir on these ships," the chairman said. "Just chairman is fine."

Benny nodded, looking around at the large and comfortable office. "I'm back on the ship I presume?"

"You are," the chairman said. "Are you interested in joining us, I hope?"

"Benny wants to know more about Seeders history and what we do and why," Gina said. "Before he makes up his mind."

Benny nodded to that.

"Sensible," the chairman said. "But I do hope you decide to join us. We can use all the help we can get in the mess below."

"I'm going to help with that," Benny said, "even if I don't join your people."

"Of that I have no doubt," the chairman said. "But we need help in the long-term planning to get the survivors back into full civilization as soon as possible, and that's what we really need the help with."

"You're thinking years down the road already?" Benny asked, kind of stunned.

"Decades and centuries," the chairman said.

Benny didn't even know what to think about that.

Then the chairman turned to Gina. "You thinking basic overall lesson?"

"I am," Gina said. "Won't take more than an hour, but will give Benny all the information he needs to decide without me trying to explain it all."

"You have my permission," he said.

He reached out and shook Benny's hand again. "I hope we can talk soon."

"Thank you, Chairman," Gina said.

"Yes, thank you," Benny said.

A moment later they were standing in a very comfortable apartment. A thin blanket lay scattered on a couch, paperwork covered a coffee table along with some dirty dishes.

He could see a dining table and a kitchen beyond.

Everything was in brown tones and photos of beautiful natural scenes were scattered along the walls, some of which looked slightly alien in nature.

"This is my apartment," Gina said.

"On the ship?" Benny asked.

"On the ship," Gina nodded. "Sorry for the mess. It was a rough few days getting ready to join you."

Benny actually liked that the apartment looked lived in. If it had been spotless, he would have worried.

She led the way into a side office with three large screens and a comfortable chair.

She tapped a spot on the desktop and the screens came alive. She dropped into the chair like she had done so for a very long time, her fingers moving over a panel he could barely see in front of her.

The image of the main area in the Empire State Building came up. The boys and the professor were still watching television.

Gina's hands moved and she quickly checked in on Candice. She was sound asleep.

Then Gina pulled the image back out so it felt like a plane over New York. The city was dotted with green lights.

Gina shook her head, then sadly she said. "We lost three more today."

"How many are there on the island now?" Benny asked, kneeling down beside her so he could see her screen clearly.

The four green dots in the Empire State Building were clear. And in another high rise building about twenty blocks to the north there were another seven green dots.

The rest were scattered, mostly solo.

Benny didn't want to think about being alone in all that smell. Survival, or any reason for survival, would seem like a distant thought. They had to help some of these people.

Gina quickly cleared the board and brought up another screen. Then in a drawer to her right she dug out two ear buds.

She stood and gestured for him to sit in the chair.

He did, feeling odd being in her chair.

She handed him the two ear buds. "Put those in your ears and face the main screen."

"What will happen?" he asked.

"Over about an hour you will be given all the history we know of the Seeders, what we can all do as far as skills, what you would need to do to join, and our mission statement. All that basic stuff."

"So I just sit and watch?"

She nodded. "It will feed you the information as fast as you can absorb it. It mostly takes about an hour. At least that's what it took for me. You won't feel the time going by."

"What will you be doing?" he asked.

"Cleaning my apartment," she said, smiling. "And doing some dishes."

"Can't say I'm not scared about this," he said.

"Just think of it as a movie without popcorn."

He took a deep breath, moving his shoulders and neck around, then exhaled. She remembered how scared she had been with this first introduction. But after that, she hadn't been afraid at all.

"I'm ready," he said, putting the two ear buds in.

"See you shortly," she said.

Then she pressed the start button.

Chapter Thirty-eight

GINA PUSHED the button and saw the images start to flash past in front of Benny. He didn't stiffen or anything, just sat there, staring straight ahead.

He was incredibly handsome. She could just stare at him, and she had a hard time believing he was really sitting here in her office, in her apartment, on the ship.

She sure hoped he decided to join the Seeders.

She was starting to wonder what this future job would be like without him working with her.

She turned and headed for the door. Her apartment needed a good cleaning and the dishes would start smelling if she didn't do something with them soon. This hour was as good a time as any to do that.

She was almost out the door when behind her Benny said, "Wow, that was something."

She spun around and went back to her screens as he pushed back and pulled the ear buds out.

She quickly checked the program. It had run completely.

He had absorbed that entire program in less than three minutes.

How was that possible?

"You all right?" she asked as he put the buds on the desktop.

"I'm fine, and impressed," he said. "Can't imagine why a group like the Seeders would want a city boy from a backwards planet to join up. But it sure has some nice perks, from what I can tell."

She opened her mouth, than shut it, then opened it again, then shut it again.

He looked at her. "Is there something wrong?"

"I honestly don't know," she said, her stomach twisting and fear clamping down on her stomach.

"Chairman Carson, permission to talk with you?" she said into the air.

"Granted," he said.

"Something's wrong, isn't it?" Benny asked, worry filling his eyes.

"We'll find out in a minute," she said, and transported them to the chairman's office.

He seemed to be surprised that Benny was with her. When they both appeared, he frowned.

"Change your mind?" the chairman asked.

"Actually, no," Benny said, smiling. "I'm pretty convinced I like what I saw."

The chairman glanced at Gina and she nodded.

"Three minutes," she said.

"Holy shit," the chairman said.

Then the chairman looked up slightly. "Chairman Ray, would it be possible for you to join me?"

A moment later Gina was stunned again as one of the most powerful and oldest of all Seeders appeared in the room. He glanced at Chairman Carson, then strode over and extended his hand. "My name is Chairman Wade Ray."

"Benny Slade," Benny said. "Nice to meet you."

Chairman Ray looked at Benny and stepped back. "Have you decided to join us?"

"Just took the introduction video," Benny said. "I want to sleep on it, but I like what I've seen so far."

"He did the introduction video in three minutes," Gina said.

Benny looked at her. "I thought you said it was going to take me an hour."

"It took me an hour," she said, smiling at him, but she couldn't make her stomach stop worrying about what this might mean.

"It takes most people an hour," Chairman Ray said, smiling. "But not all. Just as your memory could not be wiped clear of your time on the ship, the Seeder gene you carry is so strong, it allowed you to absorb that lesson almost instantly."

"And what exactly does that mean?" Benny asked, clearly as worried as Gina felt.

"It means I hope very much you decide to join us," Chairman Ray said, smiling.

"And if I did, would I be able to stay here and help my planet recover?" Benny asked.

"We would desperately need you to do just that," Chairman Ray said. "And help us all plan the future recovery."

Benny nodded and Gina let out a sigh of relief. There was real hope that Benny would join the Seeders.

"Do me a favor, would you?" Chairman Ray asked Benny. "You saw in the training how Seeders can jump from one spot to another? And I assume Ms. Helm has shown you as well."

Benny nodded.

Chairman Ray stepped back closer to the wall. "Imagine yourself standing here beside me looking at Ms. Helm."

"I'm not sure what you mean?" Benny asked.

"Just believe you are standing beside me, facing Gina Helm. Close your eyes and try it for me once. Just believe you are here."

Gina watched as Benny shrugged. She had no idea what Chairman Ray was trying to do.

Benny closed his eyes and a moment later he was standing beside Chairman Ray.

Gina covered her mouth to not allow the gasp to come out.

Benny opened his eyes and staggered back against the wall in shock, shaking one of Chairman Carson's pictures, but not knocking it down.

"Did you do that?" Benny asked.

Chairman Ray just shook his head and smiled. "You are a natural Seeder, the gene is so strong in you. There are four others like you on this planet. We made sure all four survived and none of them remember the rescue because we had spotted them ahead of time and kept them knocked out. We didn't find you until the transport."

Gina opened her mouth and then shut it. She had no idea what to say or even what it meant for a Seeder to have a strong gene. She didn't even know Seeders had special genes until earlier today.

"Is this normal to have five naturals on one developing planet?" Chairman Carson asked.

"So far, this is the only five we have found in this galaxy," Chairman Ray said.

Then he looked at Gina. "No one told you, but you were a natural as well, only one of two in your galaxy so far. We hid that information from you because at that point we didn't know what to do."

Gina could feel her mouth opening, then closing.

She wanted to breathe, but doubted she could at the moment. She had no idea what it meant to be a natural, but she was stunned that Chairman Ray and others had known about her and followed her.

Chairman Ray smiled. "I would say you two have a lot to talk about. I hope you will take our formal training, Benny Slade. I have a hunch it won't take long."

"What would happen if I decided to do so," Benny asked.

Chairman Ray smiled. "Then I would personally help both you and Gina develop to your full potential so you could help us save this planet."

Gina could say nothing. Her mind was gone.

Chairman Ray knew about her when she was recruited. She kept thinking about that over and over. She didn't feel special, at least no more than any other Seeder.

Chairman Ray nodded to them, then to Chairman Carson.

And then he vanished.

Gina just wanted her mind to return. One solid thought.

Anything.

"How far away is he going right now?" Benny asked, staring at the spot where Chairman Ray had been.

"No telling," Chairman Carson said. "Across the galaxy, maybe. A couple hundred thousand light years, maybe. No way of knowing."

Benny laughed. "At some point I really need to learn how far both of those measurements are."

Chapter Thirty-nine

BENNY HAD NO IDEA what had happened, exactly, in the chairman's office, or even who this Chairman Wade Ray was. The guy seemed important, but Benny would have to ask Gina later about that.

But right now Gina seemed as stunned as he was feeling.

The training information was now in his mind and he could remember it all when he focused on it.

He knew Seeders were humans that went from galaxy to galaxy seeding the human race on Earth-like planets. And then hundreds of thousands of Seeders remained behind the front line to help out the planted humans advance and get past all the self-destruction points to become advanced democratic cultures.

Many Seeders just remained and settled on the planets they helped, others, like Gina, moved around.

There was no information about any sort of "natural seeder" people in the introduction program. Not a word.

However, it had talked some about the ability of Seeders to transport, but it said in the video that took training. Seemed he could do that already. It scared him to think about that. Training sounded like a damned good idea when it came to jumping all over the place.

Gina, after a moment, seemed to recover slightly and nodded to Chairman Carson. "We'll talk with you soon, I'm sure."

The chairman nodded and Gina jumped them to her apartment.

Again he was impressed on how comfortable her apartment felt, but he really wanted to be back in the city.

"How about we go to our apartments on the surface?" Benny said. "I think I need to be a little grounded."

Gina nodded. "Two to transport to the surface," she said in the general direction of the ceiling. At some point he'd ask her why she did that.

A moment later they were standing in Benny's living room.

Around them, out the windows, the once bright city was dark, only shadows of buildings like ghosts in the summer night. Overhead the stars were bright, filling the summer sky. More than likely this was one of the first times the stars could be seen from downtown Manhattan in a hundred years.

He knew those stars out there were full of humans. The idea of that just stunned him.

And after he helped this planet recover, he could go out there if he wanted to.

The idea of that flat scared him more than he wanted to admit.

He moved over to the kitchen area and pulled out a popcorn maker and started it up.

Gina had not said a word since they got back. She had gone around and sat down on the couch staring out into the dark night and all the stars beyond the windows.

He poured them both a glass of white wine, even though he wasn't sure if she even liked wine, and walked over and set both glasses down on the coffee table in front of her.

Then, saying nothing, he went back to the kitchen area to wait for the popcorn to pop. He was pretty sure she hadn't even noticed him.

Finally, when he had a large bowl done and two glasses of ice water as well, he went back to the couch and sat down a little distance from her.

He put the green plastic bowl of popcorn between them. It smelled wonderful and he had salted it, again without asking if she liked popcorn or salt on popcorn.

He set her glass of water beside her untouched glass of wine, then leaned back sort of sideways on the couch so he could see her beautiful face. Her gaze was distant, not really in the room. He had no idea what she was thinking about, but he needed to find out.

And he needed some answers as well.

"Mind telling me who this Chairman Ray person is?"

She seemed to come back into her eyes at that point, then nodded.

She took a drink of water, then seemed to see the wine for the first time when she set her water glass down. She picked up the wine and sipped it.

"This is good," she said. "Thanks."

He took a drink of wine as well, then a handful of popcorn, waiting for her to answer his question.

"As far as I know," she said, holding the wine in her hands, "Chairman Ray is one of the oldest and most powerful of all Seeders. No one knows how old he really is, but he and his wife are rumored to be maybe two hundred thousand years old, if not more."

Benny had the popcorn half-chewed when she said that. His mind told him from the information he had gotten in the training program that extreme long age was possible. But grasping that kind of age was far, far beyond him.

He was still having issues with the fact that Gina was two hundred years old.

"Powerful how?" Benny asked, pushing the age part back. "My understanding from the training thing is that there is no real organization that runs the Seeders."

"That's true," Gina said, "as far as I know. But with age comes respect and the oldest tend to help plan things. But realize, I haven't had much more Seeder history than what you got earlier."

"So I have some special Seeder gene, more so than most Seeders, and it seems so do you," Benny said. "Any idea exactly what that means?"

"Not a clue," she said. "I wish I did. I didn't even know there was such a thing as a Seeder gene until they told me that was the reason you could remember the ship."

Benny realized that in the training program he had gone through, there was not one word about that either.

"So we're both kind of flying in the dark here," he said.

"Pitch dark," she said.

She took another sip of wine and nodded. "You would think after two hundred years, this kind of thing wouldn't happen to me. I feel like I did when I was approached to be a Seeder. Confused and puzzled."

"Good," he said. "That makes two of us."

She laughed and set her wine down and took a handful of popcorn. After she tasted a handful she smiled. "Perfect."

"So do you think I should join?" he asked. "Get the training?"

"That's up to you," she said.

"Have you ever regretted it?"

"Not for an instant," she said.

"So I know it's my decision," Benny said. "But I could use your opinion."

"My personal opinion is that I want you to join for selfish reasons," she said. "I want to work with you, get to know you better, and save a lot of people with you."

"Some of that doesn't sound so selfish," he said. "But we can do that without me joining."

"For a while," she said, nodding. "But I have a hunch if you could do some of the things I can do, and we both get whatever advanced training Chairman Ray is talking about, we will be even more effective. And save even more people."

Benny glanced out over the dark city. He remembered clearly those green lights on the screen in Gina's apartment on the ship. Each person, each green light, needed help. And some needed it quickly or they would not survive for long.

He had to make this decision quickly. And then get on with the job at hand.

"Let me sleep on this for the night," he said. "And I'll have a decision in the morning."

"Good idea," she said, nodding.

"But honestly," he said, "I'm leaning toward signing up."

When he said that, it felt right.

She smiled. "I hope you keep leaning."

"So one more question and then we can relax and watch a movie or something," he said.

"Anything," she said.

"How far is a light year?"

She looked at him for a moment, then laughed. "Light travels at one-hundred-and-eighty-six thousand miles per second."

He nodded. He remembered that from school somewhere.

"A light year is how far light travels in one year's time," she said.

And once again he couldn't imagine that distance. He got the thousands part.

He shook his head. "Some way to relay to me how big this galaxy is?" he said.

"There are billions of stars in this galaxy. Many billions."

He nodded, looking out at the stars.

"If this planet was represented by one speck of dust here on the coffee table," she said. "Using that scale of this planet as a speck of dust, this galaxy would be far, far, far bigger than this planet."

"And there are a lot of galaxies?" he asked, trying to even pretend to grasp that much distance.

"Billions," she said.

And once again he couldn't imagine the size and scale. "I think I'm going to need one of your learning programs to actually understand any of this. Sorry I asked."

She laughed, moved the popcorn bowl to the table and came over and leaned against him, putting her head against his chest and stretching out on the couch.

Damn that felt good.

And it felt right.

And tomorrow when he woke up he knew what decision he was going to make.

He was joining this beautiful woman. In every way he could.

Chapter Forty

GINA AWOKE the next morning to the smell of bacon and toast cooking.

The sun was just coming up over the city and the sky was a deep blue. The water around the island looked calm and a dark gray, contrasting with the metal and steel and stone of the giant structures around them.

This city was a beautiful place, of that there was no doubt. She could see why Benny loved it so much.

Last night she and Benny had tried to watch a movie, but both of them had fallen asleep.

Benny woke her up after a short time and got her headed to her own bed in her apartment. She had made some groggy mention that she would like to sleep with him and he had said they both needed the sleep. And if she slept with him, neither of them would sleep.

She had known he was right.

And now, after sleeping, she did feel rested.

A moment later there was a knock on her door.

"Come in," she said, sitting up in bed and working to straighten out her bed hair. She had slept in a t-shirt and a pair of running shorts.

"Breakfast in ten minutes," he said, smiling at her.

Her heart damn near beat out of her chest. He was more attractive than before, if that was possible, standing there in his jeans, dress shirt with the sleeves rolled up, and a yellow plastic spatula in one hand.

"Smells wonderful," she said.

"Do you drink coffee?" he asked.

"I do," she said. "Black. Do I have time for a quick shower?"

"Make it real quick if you want warm eggs and toast," he said, smiling.

Then he turned away and headed back to the kitchen.

Eleven minutes later, showered and wearing jeans and a thin blue blouse with a sports bra under it, she padded into his kitchen with her shoes and socks in hand.

He was just serving up two eggs, light toast, and a slice of ham for each plate. He also had what looked to be orange juice in glasses at the table.

"I told the professor we were going to have breakfast up here," he said as she took her seat and he slid the plate in front of her.

The food smelled heavenly and she dug into the slice of ham, letting the slightly salty taste melt in her mouth.

He sat across from her, eating as well, and they didn't speak for a few minutes until finally he said, "I've decided to join up. I can see no reason not to and about a thousand reasons to join."

She smiled, then stood and went around the table and kissed him, long and hard.

Just about the point where neither of them were going to finish their breakfasts, she pulled away and went back to her side of the table. She barely made it back. She really just wanted to make love to him right there.

He was smiling and she could feel that she was as well.

"How long will this training take?" he asked.

"Not a clue," she said. She pointed out over the city. "We don't have a lot of time for some of the people out there."

"I was thinking that," he said. "So after breakfast let's ask and then get to work."

"We'll do it from my office in the ship first," she said, "find the person who needs the most help soonest and get there."

"I was going to suggest the same thing," he said.

He finished his breakfast and pushed the plate away, taking one last sip of orange juice.

She did the same and they stood together.

"Door is still locked," he said, "and the professor won't be expecting us down there for a good hour or two."

She nodded. "Let's go find out what this training is all about."

She reached out and took his hand and he held it, his grasp firm in her hand, his skin wonderful against hers.

"Chairman Carson, would you contact Chairman Ray? Benny and I are ready to go."

"Wonderful," Chairman Carson said after a moment. "My office."

"You ready?" she asked Benny."

"Scared to death and I have a ton of doubts," he said. "Sort of like climbing on the old roller coaster on Coney Island back in the day. So why not?"

She nodded and squeezed his hand, not really knowing what he meant.

"I'm worried as well, but not scared of what's coming. I know it can only be good if we do it together."

"Now that I agree with," he said.

She again squeezed his hand and said, "Two to transport aboard."

Then a moment later she had them standing in Chairman Carson's office facing a smiling Chairman Wade Ray.

Chapter Forty-one

BENNY SMILED at the man with the long, gray hair and the broad smile.

"I'm ready to go, Chairman," Benny said. He indicated Gina. "We both are. Together."

Ray nodded. "That is fantastic to hear."

"How long is this training going to take?" Gina asked. "We have a lot of hurting people in that city below we need to get to and rescue."

Ray smiled, but his eyes were serious and Benny could tell that saving people was important to Ray. "Twenty minutes for the training, maybe another hour for me to answer your basic questions."

Benny nodded. They could take that time. It would be more than worth it, he had a hunch.

"We can do that," Gina said.

"We'll need to go to my ship in this galaxy first and pick up my wife Tacita," Ray said. "Then we will jump to another ship for the training."

Benny had no idea exactly what Ray meant, but he had a hunch he would in an hour or so.

Gina nodded. "Let's get started."

Chairman Ray glanced at the silent Chairman Carson. "We will return in an hour or so."

Carson only nodded.

A moment later Benny found himself standing on what looked like a conference room in a building. It had no windows and only a long table surrounded by leather chairs that were pushed in. There were photos on the wall of various stars and beautiful images of colored clouds in space.

A woman with long black hair appeared next to Ray.

Ray said, "My wife, Chairman Tacita."

"An honor to meet you," Gina said, bowing slightly.

"Yes, an honor," Benny said, nodding toward the woman with the dark eyes and a slight smile.

Ray took Tacita's hand and a moment later they were standing on a massive

Now Available
from all your favorite booksellers
in trade paper and electronic editions.

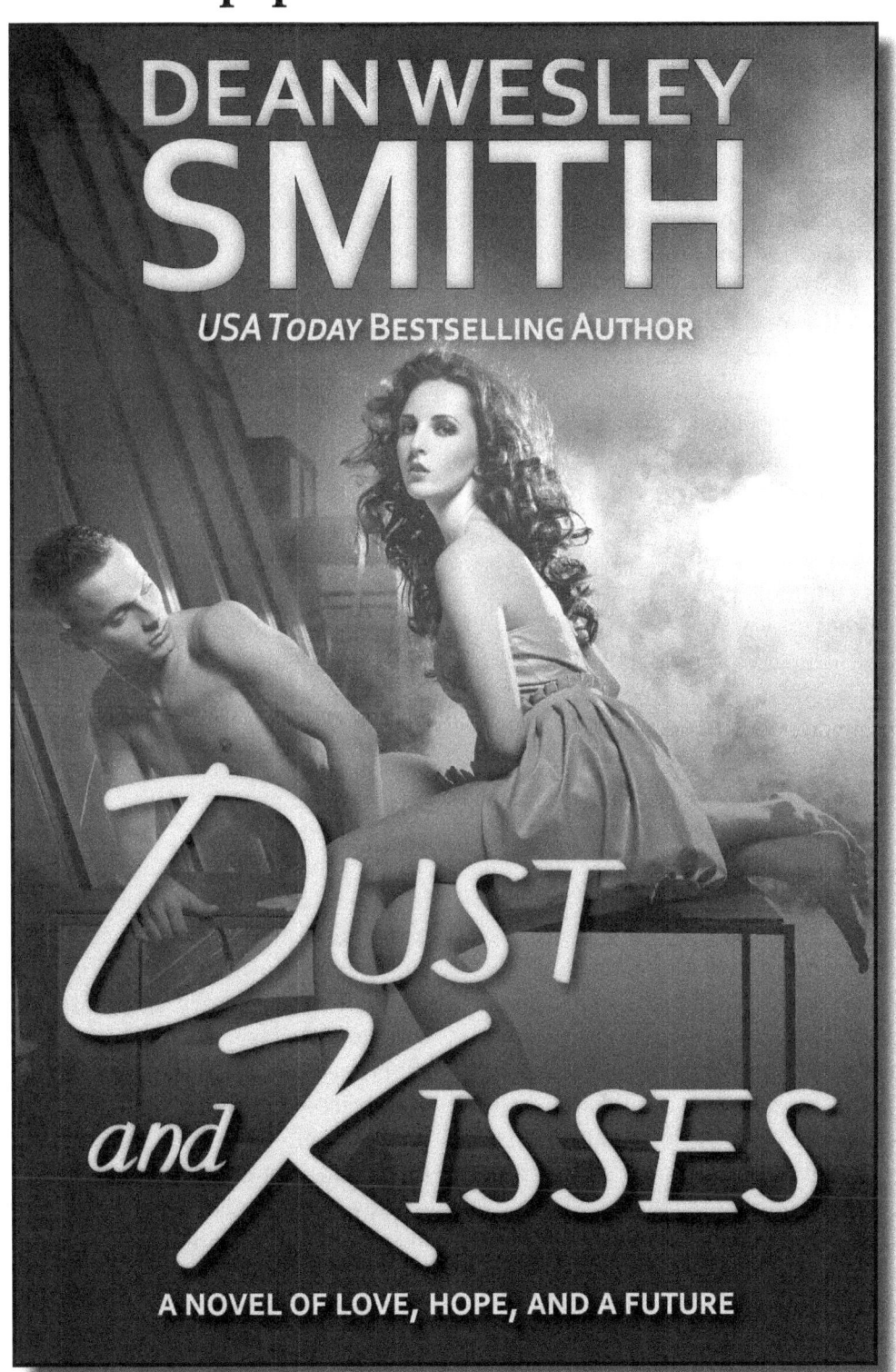

control area of a ship. A good dozen people manned stations around the room the size of a small gym. And two white chairs molded together and facing front were down two levels.

Benny couldn't hear a thing. Everyone worked in silence at their stations, not even noticing that four people had arrived.

"Where are we?" Gina asked.

"This is the control bridge of our main ship," Ray said. "We are, at the moment, about seventy galaxies away from the Milky Way Galaxy."

Gina staggered a little and Benny put out his arm to hold her. She clearly understood distances. Maybe it was better, for the moment, that he didn't really understand just how far they had jumped in that instant of time.

"I've never seen a ship this size," Gina said after a moment.

"There are none this size in the Milky Way," Tacita said, her voice flat and matter-of-fact, "and won't be for another three hundred years."

"But two are on their way there now," Ray said.

Benny had no idea what any of this meant, but he had to admit that if this was just the control room of a ship, how huge was the ship itself? He didn't figure they would have time for a tour, since all this was only supposed to take just over an hour.

Ray led them over to two chairs against a far wall facing two large screens and indicated that they should sit.

Gina did and Benny found himself only hesitating for a moment before sitting down as well.

The chair looked like a hard plastic, but it molded around him and supported his back perfectly as he sat down. Nice invention.

"Please put both hands on the surface in front of you," Ray said.

Benny did at the same time Gina did beside him.

And that was the last thing he remembered about being in that large bridge until Chairman Ray said that they could sit back.

He felt like he had just had every bit of information in the New York City Library forced into his brain, organized, and stored.

And so, so much more.

He knew that now he was a Seeder. In all respects.

He stood and Gina slowly stood beside him, her hand on his arm for support.

Then Benny looked up into the eyes of Chairman Ray and Chairman Tacita and bowed slightly. He knew them, he knew that they were much, much older than even rumored, that this ship they were on was the first Seeder Mother Ship, and so much more.

"Thank you for this honor," Benny said. And he meant it. More than he had ever meant anything in his life.

"Yes, thank you," Gina said, and she also bowed slightly.

A moment later the four of them were in a very comfortable lounge with four chairs and light crackers and cheeses and glasses of water on a wooden coffee table in the center. Each chair was an overstuffed brown leather chair and as Benny sat, again the chair formed comfortably around him.

After all four of them were seated, Chairman Ray said, "That process took exactly twenty-one minutes. You have been gone now from Chairman Carson's ship for just under thirty minutes. I know time is of the essence to you at this point in the rescue, but I hope you will take this next hour to ask us any question you feel is necessary."

Benny looked over at Gina and she nodded.

"We can take the time," he said.

Benny now understood exactly how far they were from his New York City and the Milky Way Galaxy. He just understood it. He wasn't sure how, but he understood it now and was impressed. But he had one question he still didn't understand.

"All Seeders have a Seeder gene," Benny said. "What makes the one we have so special? Does it give us extra powers?"

Ray smiled. "Not so much, but in a way, yes. You can remember things over centuries better than others and you both have the ability to transport vast distances, far greater distances than any normal Seeder."

"But the biggest factor is that the gene," Tacita said, "gives you the ability to chairman with a partner one of these mother ships."

"Oh," Benny said, sitting back. In his mind the size of a Seeder mother ship was clear. They were as large as most moons. And could carry millions of people.

"Wow," Gina said.

They talked for another thirty minutes, Benny just confirming basic knowledge he had in his mind more than anything else.

Finally he said something that had been bothering him, because he knew that Seeders, especially Seeders like Ray and Tacita, never did much of anything without a plan.

"So with me and Gina now working on my home world, that makes six of us there, four you saved from the disaster twice."

"Actually," Ray said, "Since yesterday we found yet another who survived. And another showed up just after the last wave hit from another local planet. They have teamed up and both are being recruited."

"So eight there," Benny said. "What is it, the water?"

"We honestly don't know," Tacita said.

"So what is your plan for all of us?"

"We want you all to help save the population of your planet first and foremost," Ray said, "along with thousands of other Seeders helping out around your planet."

"But after that is stable?" Benny asked, leaning forward.

Ray smiled. "We hope you and Gina in a few years will recruit the other four."

"We can do that," Benny said. "And then what?"

"If we could see into the future," Tacita said, "we would."

"But we can't," Ray said smiling.

Benny nodded. He knew that, for the moment, Ray and Tacita didn't want to talk about any possible plans. And that honestly made sense to Benny. He and Gina needed to concentrate on saving lives.

And finding a new way for people on his Earth to live going forward.

Benny stood and Gina did as well, slightly ahead of Ray and Tacita.

"It's time we get started," Benny said.

"I agree," Ray said.

Ray reached over and took Tacita's hand and an instant later they were back in Chairman Carson's office.

Carson jumped to his feet and bowed slightly to all of them.

"I'm glad you have joined us," Ray said to Benny. "Good luck in this coming battle."

"Yes," Tacita said. "Best success."

And with that they were both gone.

Benny glanced at the startled face of Chairman Carson. "Thank you, Chairman, for the use of your office."

"Yes, thank you," Gina said.

"Any time," Carson said.

"Shall we go to work?" Benny asked Gina.

"Let's do it," she said, giving him that smile he was coming to love more than anything.

A moment later, side-by-side, they were bent over a screen in her apartment office, their shoulders touching as they studied the green dots and the notes Gina had made about each person.

Even though Benny now understood the vast expanse of human worlds out there in the stars, even though this was his first day as a Seeder, his only focus was on his home city, his home planet, and saving as many people as he could as quickly as he could.

There would be time later to really think about what had happened. And what he had agreed to.

The larger Seeders Universe would take time for him to understand. But many people out there in his home city amid all the death didn't have time.

So he was focused.

And he knew that the woman of his dreams beside him felt exactly the same way.

They needed to quickly find survivors.

And then together rescue them.

After all, saving human life, human cultures, was what Seeders did.

He was now a Seeder. And that felt exactly right.

The First Four Seeders Universe Novels
Available at your favorite booksellers.

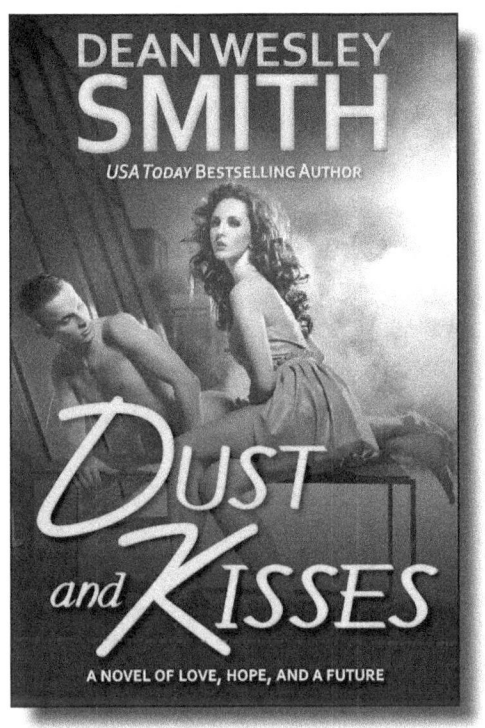

#1... October 2013

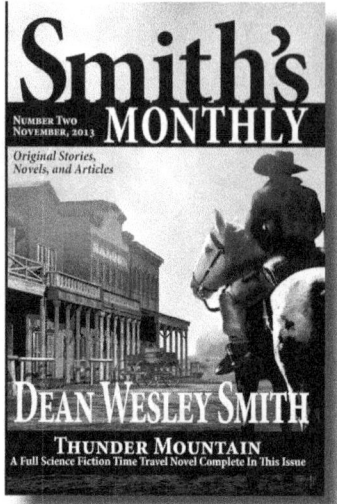

#2... November 2013

#3... December 2013

#4... January 2014

#5... February 2014

#6... March 2014

The First Full Year of Smith's Monthly!!!

Subscribe Now and start with any issue.

All are also available from all your favorite booksellers
in trade paper and electronic editions.

#7... April 2014

#8... May 2014

#9... June 2014

#10... July 2014

#11... August 2014

#12...September 2014

Don't Miss an Issue!

Subscribe

Electronic Subscription:
6 Issues... $29.99
12 Issues... $49.99

Paper Subscription:
6 Issues... $59.99
12 Issues... $99.99

And Continuing into Year #2. Don't Miss an Issue!

#13...October 2014

Poems by DEAN WESLEY SMITH

Pipe Dreams

Belief in yourself runs strong
through creations…
        conceptions…
           ideas…

All encased in gold.

"Fools gold," they say, laughing
and snickering.
"No chance."
      "No Way."
        "Never Work."

And you argue, "But, maybe…"
or "What if?"
Seeing goals
      possibilities,
          maybe even a future.

"That's crazy," they say,
closed minds closing down
in disgust.
     "It's never been done."
       "It sure won't work."

And so it goes…

The dreams, the beliefs dim
flicker and fade
with each opposing sentence,
     now contained neatly in lists of things
       you must think about before…

Your dreams and beliefs,
pushed and shoved by ridicule,
smashed by laughter,
     are finally filed by a coward
       in a drawer labeled dreams.